Tahiti Blues

Alex W. Du PREL

TAHITI BLUES

Modern tales of the South Seas

Les Editions de Tahiti
Moorea, French Polynesia, South Pacific

All contents copyright © 2011 by Alex W. DuPREL/ Les Editions de Tahiti.
ISBN 978-2-907776-38-7

Cover art by **Philippe DUBOIS**, *artiste peintre* living on the island of Moorea.

Eternal thanks to Kahaia and Poema,
For a life full of Polynesian serendipity.

Table of Contents

Teiki, Tahitian Diver   7

Francesco   31

An Outstanding Pearl   41

Island Sorrow   59

A Subject of Her Majesty the Queen   63

The Ghost of The Palace Hotel   77

Deep Metal   95

Marlon's Tahiti Blues   101

The Author   128

Teiki, Tahitian Diver

ET me tell you a story that took place in the Tuamotu Archipelago, this magnificent chain of atolls that stretches out more than a thousand miles East of Tahiti.

What you shall read now happened on one of these islands, these fragile sand bars studded with a few coconut trees that surround emerald blue lagoons. The name of this atoll is Tangatoa. It is located some four hundred miles from Papeete, the capital of Tahiti. It is well known for the quality of its pearls and for the friendliness of its people.

This is where Mark built his hotel. This is where Teiki pushes his wheelbarrow and laughs every time he sees Mark.

This story is not Mark's story. That one we shall tell another time, for Mark is quite a picturesque person. Absolute master of his small hotel lost at the end of the world, Mark's main occupation is an endless shuttle between his hammock and the bar.

Once in a while, some intrepid tourist dares to upset this routine. It is actually a total disrespect for the classic laws of inn-keeping that helped make his enterprise a success. A total indifference for the wishes of customers crazy enough to go five hundred miles out of their way only to be ignored by the manager of the only resort on the island.

But, after a day of observation, and if Mark considers you worthy of his interest, he will really go out of his way to make you discover the spirit and the gentleness of these islands. The endless beaches with nobody on them. The fantastic colors of the reef. The most beautiful vahine. Well, a whole new world you never would have dared imagine.

It was my third visit. The hot noon sun chased us toward the shade of the bar. I'm telling Mark the latest Papeete gossip.

Suddenly, next to us, appears a well-built Polynesian. Quite proud, but pleasant. He is pushing a wheelbarrow full of dry leaves, a rake on top. I recognize Teiki. He sets the barrow down and we greet each other with joy. Afterward, he picks up his barrow and goes on his way. Laughing.

"He really gets on my nerves; he really bugs me!" says Mark.

"Why does he laugh like that?"

"I don't really know. It's quite a long story. Have lunch with me, and I'll tell you what happened. Maybe you'll be able to figure out what's the matter with him."

An hour later, we sat down for lunch. Titine brought a huge dish of lagoon jack fish, certainly one of the best tasting fishes anywhere in the world. Mark helped himself, pushed the plate my way and started telling me the story of Teiki, the Paumotu (native of the Tuamotu) :

"Teiki was born here on Tangatoa, more than forty years ago. His mother, then a fifteen-year old beauty, had surrendered to the charm of a tall tattooed Marquesan. He was a sailor on Won-Cha's boat, the Chinaman's sailing schooner that used to cruise the northern group to trade mother-of-pearl shells for general goods. And which also introduced the first movies to the islands. In those days you just stretched a bed sheet between two coconut trees at dusk, brought ashore a projector and a small generator, and you were in business. The 'entrance' fee was a mother-of-pearl shell. Everybody arrived with a woven pandanus mat to sit on in the sand while watching the movie. Which was usually some old Western or corny love story.

"What beautiful memories these days bring back. Everybody would just scream during deep kissing shots, an unknown custom to the islanders then. Or weep with big sniffs during sad scenes. The films shown were either in French or in English, neither languages people here really understood. And it could happen that the reels got mixed up, like the first reel being shown last.

But it didn't matter. Most people spoke only the Paumotu dialect then anyhow. The real celebration was that there was a movie. The only window to the outside world. The only entertainment.

"The Chinaman bought the mother-of-pearl for a pittance, and sold the rice and bully beef dearly. The natives were aware of it. But the joy of watching a movie, seeing something different, made them forget. Beside marriages and funerals, the showing was the great social event. Everyone was there. Even the old and the sick were carried over by relatives.

"Let's get back to Teiki.

Thus, he is a keepsake the strong Marquesan had left his mother. The sailor had fascinated and charmed the young girl with stories of his many voyages. To Papeete. To Christmas Island. To the Cook Islands. To Bora Bora at the time of the American base, where he even saw airplanes.

She gave him a beautiful baby. Our Teiki. The Marquesan was a nice man. He never beat her. He always brought colorful *pare'u*s (lava-lavas) when passing through. She was really happy and proud of him. Until the schooner returned one day without him. The island never heard of him again. Maybe he drowned in some shipwreck. Or left for Noumea to work in the nickel mines. Or just started a new family somewhere on Tahiti.

"She waited for more than a year. She then gave the baby to her mother to keep and went to Papeete to live there for a couple of years. Most of our island girls do that. It is better for them to have fun and see the city lights before settling into a permanent partnership. That way they acquire the experience to satisfy and keep their husbands. And if they come back with a child, it only shows proof of their fertility.

"So, when she returned to Tangatoa, she took back Teiki, her son, and a few months later moved in with Teremu, the island postmaster. Teremu was one of the sought-after bachelors on the island, because of his steady salary. But even better, his family held the fishing rights on the entrance of the pass. Our postmaster was actually much more a fisherman, as the mail boat called on an average of only once a month. And his grandfather had built a whole system of these ingenious fish traps in the pass that catch the fish by themselves.

"You may wonder why I'm telling you all this. I know you are quite familiar with the islands. But to understand Teiki, like anything else down here, one needs a bit of patience. We have lots of time anyhow and I love to speak.

â€œSo Teremu accepts Teiki as his own son, which is the custom here. He teaches the young boy all the secrets of the sea, the pass and the lagoon. He teaches him how to live with the numerous sharks. How to respect them. How to understand them, how to feed them. Because the pass is full of these monsters. Even a few hammerhead sharks. All ordinary inhabitants of tropical lagoon passes.

"To kill them would not help—quite the contrary. Every shark holds his own territory, which he protects. It requires a lot of patience and time to get them used to the presence of man. Thus, if you kill these sharks, they will just be immediately replaced by others from the open sea. Real wild ones.

"This is why we do not like too much the Rambo type tourists who arrive with big bang-sticks and offer to clean the pass for us.

"Thus, since many generations, a real affinity between man and shark has established itself. Man respects the guardian of the pass and gives him part of his catch. Like paying toll. To maintain a good relationship. The shark, in exchange, patrols the pass and thus protects the lagoon and the fishermen from the predators of the open sea. Actually, our sharks are almost tame. But one must always respect them. Not take them for granted. Because they also have their pride. Just like our people.

"You know, it's a very fragile world out here. Everything is delicately balanced. Man only takes the fish he needs. He throws back the lobster with eggs. He does not cut the young coconut tree to eat the heart.

"An atoll is just like a small planet. A miracle of nature, very fragile. Any excess will be followed by a disaster. Look at the mother-of-pearl : If you over-fish, soon you have none left. If you raise too many, the lagoon gets sick. It happened lately on the atoll of Takapoto, where too many pearl farms established themselves. You can see for yourself the disasters of some Society Island lagoons. Clams fished with crowbars, indiscriminate dredging, reefs choked by mud from real estate development washouts or algae feeding on pollutants. But let's not talk about such sadness—you're on vacation.

"Thus our Teiki gets the best possible training. He soon learns to become part of the lagoon. He learns to share the top of the nutrition chain with the sharks.

"When we started the pearl farm and the hotel, the island chief suggested I use Teiki as diver. Partly because he happened to be his nephew, but mostly because of his thorough knowledge of the underwater world.

"Teiki installed all the shell racks for the pearl farm by himself. A Tahitian from the fisheries department taught him how to use scuba gear. How to decompress properly while coming up.

"Teiki, like all Paumotu people, is very aware of the hazards involved with diving. The danger of the bends. The nitrogen narcosis you get from rising too fast from the deep. It is called *taravana* in our islands. It means crazy, nuts. Every village has at least one case of *taravana*. Some partially paralyzed man, or one who gets crazy fits once in a while. Diving incidents were quite frequent in the past. Especially in the early fifties, when mother-of-pearl started to become scarce. The men had to dive deeper and deeper to get their quota filled. Free diving, of course; scuba was a luxury item in those days.

"You may laugh at this, but it is the lowly plastic button, introduced then, that saved our lagoons from being totally depleted. It depressed the price of the shells and the Chinese merchants lost interest.

"Now we have our little pearl industry, of course. We have all become shell farmers and this, plus time, has more than rebuilt the stocks.

"Well, here I'm yakking away again. But it's just to explain that any kid raised on an atoll knows just about as much, if not more, about diving and the underwater world as Jacques-Yves Cousteau.

"When we opened the hotel six years ago, it was, of course, Teiki whom I put in charge of the dive shop.

"I must admit that we owe him the success of tourism on Tangatoa. Thanks to his personality. Thanks to his patience. Thanks to his kindness.

"You should have seen him, teaching city dudes to scuba dive. Especially at the beginning, when the whole world ran to the cinema to see Jaws. Try to get someone to dive among the sharks after he's seen that stupid movie. Well, Teiki did. After tons of patience and explaining. It was really touching to see the pride and joy of our guests after their first dive. Teiki had shown them how to feed the sharks in the pass, where to look for shells in the lagoon, how to fish ocean cigata. Never have I seen a customer who wasn't thrilled after an outing with Teiki. Before long, we were well known as one of the best dives in the world."

Mark took a slow sip of white wine. Then went on :

"These happy days lasted until last year; then disaster struck...

"An accident?" I asked.

"Not at all. Much worse. Wait, I'll get some fresh drinks."

Mark got up, retied his lava-lava, and walked over to the bar.

Lunch was over. The few customers had left the restaurant. The girls had cleared the tables.

The trade winds were cooling the large open building. Eight carved coconut trunks held up a roof made of thousands of woven coconut leaves. In front of me, the empty white sand beach and the lagoon. Flat as a mirror. Shimmering endless shades of blue and green.

Mark came back with two full glasses. He went on with his story :

"One day, two customers from Papeete check in. One is a *"demi"* (half breed), the other a *"Popa'a"* (white man). They book a dive for the following day.

"At dinner, I try to strike up a conversation with them. Like all of us in the islands, I love to listen to the latest Tahiti gossip. All the little secrets you do not read about in the newspapers. But they didn't loosen up. It puzzled me. Especially the silence of the demi. All local people generally talk freely and are open.

"The next morning, I watch them leave the dock with Teiki. The way they handle their gear, they seem to be experienced divers.

"They come back in time for lunch, looking happy, so I join them when the girls serve coffee and inquire about their diving trip.

- 'Very pleasant,' says the white man, 'but there is a problem.'
- 'What problem?'
- 'Your diving instructor is not licensed.'
- 'But he's Teiki. Everybody knows him...'
- 'That does not excuse him from not having a diving instructor license.'
- 'You guys have got to be kidding. We are in the Tuamotu. At the end of the world. Teiki must be one of the best diving instructors in the South Pacific. Even if he doesn't know how to read..'.

"I am so stunned that I start to speak loudly. This hadn't happened to me in years. The "Popa'a" speaks on :

- 'Sir, even in the Tuamotu, the law must be respected. The law says that any person who teaches diving must be licensed by the state. Your diver isn't. So you have to replace him. In any case, your insurance will not cover you anymore once we notify them.'

- 'Since when this law?'

- 'It was voted more than a year ago. By the Territorial Assembly. We want Tahiti and her islands islands to be a modern state. Believe me, amateurs like your Teiki will be out of fashion!'

- 'I'll send him to Papeete to pass his exam.'

- 'No sense sending him to Tahiti. There is no diving school. None in the territory. It is to France that you must send him. And I would not waste my money there either. The examinations involve long written tests about decompression tables. There is no way your illiterate Tahitian could ever even dream of obtaining a license.'

"After listening to these words, I realize that all further discussion is futile. I must go to Tahiti to straighten out this problem. I am totally appalled. Disgusted. The administrative stupidity - one reason why I had left England more than twenty years ago - had finally found me again on my lost island. It was creeping, like a cancer, into one of the last places on earth where one is still accepted for what one is. Not for the piece of paper on the wall or for the way one dresses. If someone truly deserves a PhD in oceanography, then it should be Teiki. For his knowledge of shark behavior. In his own way, of course.

"But he does not know how to read and write. He does not know what a war is. Couldn't even imagine it. He doesn't know what a Jew or an Arab is. Or a prejudice. Thus he is classified ignorant by the 'civilized' snobs. No degree. No value. Must be pushed aside. Kindness, patience, personality do not have their diplomas. You do not learn them rubbing your butt on a school bench.

"And the 'gentlemen' who vote these laws do not themselves even have a high school diploma. Such a school did not yet exist a few years ago in the islands. Won't these leaders ever realize that such laws only push their own people into a corner, marginalize them, and promote expatriates who have access to diploma mills? Any interesting job will always be solicited by some outsider with better, bigger diplomas.

"Past plagues and colonization have not succeeded in breaking the beautiful soul of the Polynesian people. But this thoughtless and heartless creeping bureaucracy may just succeed. A true cultural suicide. And all this only to create a bunch of useless public servant jobs. To do like everywhere else. To destroy one of the last alternative ways of life by smothering it with the universal mediocrity.

"When will our leaders realize that the arrogance of the consumer civilization, which states it is the best, can only impose its ways on our societies if our leaders believe this culture to be superior?

"OK. I stop. I'm getting carried away again. But every time I think about these dudes, my blood pressure just goes way up.

"Soon I'm on my way to Papeete to clear this matter. Some of my customers are councilmen or well known personalities. All have dived with Teiki. I know they will help get a dispensation.

"Well, you just won't believe it, but I did not succeed in getting one. I had arrived just before elections. Everybody was busy or laying low. 'Don't make waves,' they told me. They also said that Tangatoa was very far and had few votes, so who gives a damn ! One of them even told me that if one always gave dispensations after passing laws, they'd look like a banana republic. It was so sad to see how the mind of my friends changed once they were back in their urban environment. But I did manage to get a three month delay to be able to find a replacement for Teiki.

"You can imagine how depressed I felt when I came back home to the island. Sad to see these last shores of the end of the world slowly getting standardized. Getting to be a bad copy of other societies.

"A proud and unique people exchanging their happiness for cars and DVDs. Trading their freedom for little jobs that allow them to buy stupid gadgets. And when at night they get home tired, they sit down in front of their stupid color TV and watch some dude tell them how happy they should feel. Because they can afford all these gadgets. That they are 'civilized'. Because they can watch an average of fifty violent deaths a week in the electronic box.

"Hiro and Maui, the Polynesian heroes, have been replaced by Terminator and Rambo.

"The unique family pattern, the base of Polynesian culture, is slowly being destroyed. Replaced by the egoistic western family model. The minimum family : mom, dad and the kids. Forget your parents; they must be put in some state retirement home. Forget the rest of your family. They must be ignored. That is the only way you can afford all these material goodies. The ones they insist you must possess. To be a 'real' man. Like the man on TV.

"The proud Polynesian turned into another consumer sheep.

"When shall our leaders understand that the Polynesian cannot compete in this type of society? Because their culture is based on sharing. Why won't they learn from what happened to the American Indians or in Hawaii? Or in Guam. Or in New Zealand. And realize how much it excludes the Maori people? But that's another story. Another crusade of mine.

"Back on the island, I'm too ashamed to tell Teiki anything. I run ads in the two local papers. But my busy civil servants had hit the other resorts before mine. No more certified diving instructors available in the territory. I must run ads in France. Only this country's diplomas are now valid.

"Of course it takes time to get answers. To choose a candidate. To write back. To answer questions. So the three month delay is long gone. And Teiki is still running the dive shop.

"The "Demi" comes back. Alone. He is much more sociable this time. But explains he must give me a ticket for breaking the law. Or he might lose his overpaid job. Everyone in Papeete is, of course, aware that Teiki still takes people diving.

"This means that I have to go to court in Tahiti. I try to explain the uniqueness of the case to the judge. Try to explain that the livelihood of a whole family is in jeopardy. That Teiki is one of the best divers in the Pacific. Seven years of happy tourists with no accident attest it.

"The court listens with sweet smiles. They say the law must be the same for everyone. I insist. I question the ability of a European diver in an unknown tropical lagoon. I mention the sharks.

"People in court are polite. They answer me that licensed divers are real pros. How dare I question the value of a diploma?

"I realize my mistake. Casting a doubt on the practical value of diplomas was a frontal attack on the legal, colonial system. This army of clerks, lawyers, barristers and judges were all using degrees to justify their privileges, their cushy lives.

"So I'm the nut. The rebel. The terrorist. And please pay 20,000 francs fine. 20,000 francs only because we are nice comprehensive guys. The law is the law !

"Disgusted, I give them the money and go get drunk at the Kikiriri, the old Paumotu bar of Papeete. Man, did I ever got drunk that night.

"Then I'm stuck for a week in Papeete. All the flights to Tangatoa are booked solid. Booked with tourists who want to dive with Teiki. He who is now forbidden to show his underwater world. No diploma, not allowed to work. Real smart, the modern world. I'm getting close to a nervous breakdown. I can imagine the judges and the attorney general talking while having a drink in their air conditioned palaces : 'But my dear attorney general, one must try to understand poor Mark. He's been too long, way too long out there in these lost islands. It got to his head. Poor man ! One must pity him.' And they all nod their heads wisely.

"If they would only once get their butts out of their posh offices to see the reality of life in the outer islands, then they might realize the damage they can cause.

"Back on my lost island, I gather enough courage to tell Teiki the whole story. Impassive, he listens to me and then answers :
- 'Don't worry, boss. I'll pay back the 20 000 francs.'
- 'But you are crazy. That's not the point.'
- 'No. It's my fault. I'm the one who doesn't have a diploma.'

"So I make a long speech to explain that the fault is not his. That the city people are getting crazy. I explain that he will not be able to take guests diving alone anymore. That a man will arrive from France to go diving with him; that this man has the necessary papers. That it is only to satisfy the law. That actually nothing will change. He listens and tells me he'd like to think it over.

"He made up his mind four days later :
-'OK, Boss. Let the man come. I will show him the lot. But then I'll stop the diving trips. I've saved some money and I shall sell fish to the schooner. But I'll still dive for you on the pearl farm during grafting and harvest. If you accept. You know I like to work alone.'

"Yes, I knew very well Teiki wouldn't accept working under someone's command. Proud people are independent people. He stayed with me all these years because we have total mutual trust. Diving was his baby and I never meddled. We only discussed equipment needs or guest comments. I also knew that his decision was influenced by his concern of my having to bear two salaries for one man's work. Island resort business is survival business.

The Certified Diving Instructor was about to arrive. Teiki and I stood at the edge of the coral runway in the noon heat. Holding our flower leis.

I had some apprehensions. I do not like to hire someone unfamiliar with island mentality. Usually I only choose people who have spent at least two years among Tahitians. And then only if I cannot find a native to do the job. I do this out of respect for the island community. It is very small, thus very fragile. But I do it also out of concern for our guests, who expect to find a true island atmosphere on a far out island. They would be quite disappointed to encounter a Riviera atmosphere after traveling thousands of miles all the way to Polynesia. Our customers love to be kidded by our girls, to be talked to on an equal to equal base. Because they feel right away that the Polynesians have no idea what a "servant's mentality" is.

"Of course, once in a while, we get some bitch who demands 'service' and a few sparks fly. But I usually explain the local reasoning, and things settle down to normal. I believe more in customer education than in employee training.

"Do you know that now, on Tahiti and Moorea, they dispense employee training in some large hotels ? The same stuff they are teaching in Europe. The poor girls are taught to wear socks and shoes. To wash their feet everyday—our girls who are the cleanest in the world. That long hair is forbidden in the restaurant. That you must bow to clients. I know you won't believe it, but I have seen it personally. Thus they are being taught to lose their spontaneity and their naturalness to acquire the mind of a domestic.

"Yet the managers, the teachers and the imported staff of these new hotels do not even get a minute of training concerning the special Polynesian personality.

"Thus, instead of preserving the unique island mentality so admired everywhere, they teach our young an ethic that is not theirs. And if they imitate well this outside world, they get a nice diploma. The Good Imitator Diploma.

"But our visitors are no dupes. They want to see the real Polynesia. Not some schizophrenic population. Nobody likes copies. A Tahitian aping a European is as ridiculous as the other way around. Let's all stay at ease in our own skins... Excuse me. Here I am crusading again.

"Our new diving instructor is named Jacques. Tall, good looking, sporting type, quite pleasant, but white like an aspirin pill.

"After introductions, we all drive to the hotel in the old pick-up. Our new companion starts to talk. About his dives. About his various trips in Europe. About his past experiences. He talks and talks. He doesn't see the beautiful coconut grove. Nor the spectacular lagoon on the right. He just talks. Like a machine. Impossible to interrupt him. Even upon arrival at the hotel, he just keeps on talking. He had done everything. He knows it all. If I tried to explain something, he'd just finish my sentence for me. Atoll people are like Texas cowboys, pretty stingy with words, so Teiki and I look at each other, stunned.

"The next morning, he goes for his first dive with Teiki. Despite a few suggestions I succeeded in placing, he plays boss in front of the clients. Thus, after returning, Teiki announces that this is his last dive. He has not even been able to show the sharks to Jacques.

"Jacques wasn't a bad guy, not at all. But he was the product of a highly competitive and overpopulated society. It believed that you must impose yourself on others. That you must be a leader. That listening will be perceived as a weakness. And to show a weakness could open the door to your competitor, one of ten hungry guys waiting at the door to grab your job. Because of this permanent insecurity, Jacques resents any explanation or advice as being critical of his knowledge. Because of it, I could not reason with him. So, I made him promise to limit his dives to the lagoon proper. The pass and its sharks was off limits.

"That very same day, our gardener gave notice. He wanted to go live with his mother on another island. I offered Teiki his job. He accepted. Everybody does any type of work here. All jobs have the same social value. So far.

"Jacques quickly took charge of the dive shop. He was a hard worker. The equipment was shining. The boat and the shop spotless. The clients happy. He was slowing down, learning to blend in.

"Of course, when former customers inquired about Teiki's reconversion, I had to explain at length. Sometimes, some guests went diving privately with Teiki. After his working hours, which I kept very flexible. Jacques got jealous and complained bitterly. I replied that Teiki was free to do private diving with friends. That it did not concern the hotel. That it was legal.

"Certainly it must have been jealousy and a hurt pride that caused the drama.

"A former guest, an officer in the French Navy, arrived with his new wife. He had been raving to her about his adventures among the sharks in the pass. Talking about them for months. They came specially to Tangatoa so he could show her. Jacques explains that he doesn't dive the pass. It's too dangerous, etc... The officer calls him a chicken and other niceties of the military vocabulary.

"Deeply hurt in his pride, Jacques disobeys my orders and takes his party to the pass. In the group is also an American accountant, a novice, who thinks this is a routine dive.

"Everybody goes in the water. It's slack tide and the current is not strong. The group starts to dive.

"Once on the bottom, they see only a few lemon sharks cruising in the distance. This reassures Jacques. He decides to open a tridachnae clam to attract fish. Fish of all colors. Parrot fish. Squirrel fish. Angel fish. They come and eat right out of his hand. Jacques keeps opening clams. More and more fish come. The divers swim in a cloud of fish.

"But a hammerhead shark watches this underwater ballet from a distance. And waits for his share. But nobody brings him anything. So he decides to go get it himself.

"Suddenly, the huge shark shoots through our group of divers. Physically pushes Jacques and the girl to grab the clam. He didn't want to attack the divers. He just wanted the clam. And took off just as suddenly.

"Big panic follows. The size of the monster. His skin like sandpaper. All hell is loose. Jacques controls himself. He sees the officer and his wife going up too fast. It's a real fight to get them to stop. He gets kicked. Scratched. Bitten. Loses his mask. But he manages the impossible — calming them and getting them down again to decompress properly. No more shark around. But also no more accountant.

"Jacques searches all over. He thinks the man went up and climbed into the boat. He surfaces. Nobody in the boat. Back down. There he finds him finally. Lying behind a coral head. His regulator next to him. Dead.

"The doctor will later diagnose heart failure. From shock, fear.

"You can imagine the mess afterward ! Doctor from Rangiroa. Gendarme from Papeete. Undertaker with leaded coffin for international shipping. I'm trying to reach his family in the States via radio-telephone.

"All the village women arrive to hold a funeral singsong. All night long. They never sang so good and so loud. It was their first "Popa'a". The hotel was packed with guests who finally joined the women because the melodies were so beautiful and no one could sleep anyhow.

"Next morning, I manage to reach the sister of the dead man. His only family. She tells me outright to keep the body. To throw him in the sea, for all she cares. Funerals are expensive and she is in debt. I try to argue. I insist. But she hangs up.

"So we've got to bury him here. But there are no cemeteries. In Polynesian islands, you bury your dead at home, in front or behind your house. So we'll bury him on the hotel grounds. We'll hide the grave later with some hibiscus bush.

"I ask Teiki to dig a grave. He wants to bury the American next to his house. I refuse. He insists. He promises to take good care of the grave. Explains the dead was a diver like himself. It is a matter of pride. I finaly accept.

"This made a few people jealous. Some families came later and made me promise to give them the next "Popa'a" to die in the hotel.

"Anyhow, our accountant had a wonderful funeral. The whole island was there in their Sunday best. All hotel guests also. Both the Catholic and Protestant priests flew over from Rangiroa. I didn't know his religion. Much later I discovered that he was Jewish. But I left the cross on the grave.

"That funeral actually gave me quite a reputation. Some real snutty lady on Moorea told me the other day :
   - 'Oh, you're the one running the hotel that gives beautiful funerals.'
Whatever, everybody sang and cried for hours. He is now buried over there next to the ocean, listening to the surf forever.

"It is that day that Teiki started to laugh. Every time he would see me.

"I went to talk to him. I tried to explain the stupidity of the modern world : that the accountant is dead doesn't seem to matter. The instructor is licensed, so everything is legal. The dead have no value. The valuable thing is the fancy certificate Jacques has earned. Diving in a cold swimming pool full of chlorinated water. He never had seen a fish nore a piece of coral then. But he held a piece of paper that certifies him to be an expert diver. Everybody is happy that way. The law has been respected. The insurance pays. Even if there would have been five dead. But if Teiki dives and there are no dead, then I go to jail. Beautiful modern world. No more "amateurs".

"Teiki insists he does understand. But he keeps on laughing. And it bugs me. Really bugs me.

"0

Now that you heard the story, maybe you can explain?"

- "Ask him."

- "I tried. He won't tell me."

- "How about getting him drunk. Then he'll talk."

- "No. His wife would get sad. Or mad. She'll make a scene in front of the guests."

- "Maybe it is only you he doesn't want to tell. I'll have a few beers with him later. I'll try to find out."

That evening I am sitting with Teiki in front of a bottle. We talk about old times and the new sewing machine he bought his wife. The sun is setting over the lagoon. The three man guitar orchestra plays Tahitian songs. I feel Teiki is at ease. So I ask :

- "Say, Teiki. Why do you always laugh when you see Mark?"

He giggles, then answers :

- "I'll tell you. But you must promise not to tell him."

- "You have my word of honor."

- "OK. Here it is. You see, I'm not stupid. I laugh because Mark is a blind man. I know that two men will soon arrive from Papeete. They will ask to see my gardener's diploma. I do not have any. And Mark will have to pay another 20,000 francs."

And he then leans toward me :

- "I also know that Mark doesn't have a manager's diploma either..."

I just laugh and laugh...

Even today, Mark is still mad at me. I never told him Teiki's secret. I had promised.

As I left the next day, Teiki gave me a big wave of the hand, standing there under the trees next to his wheelbarrow. It was sad to see him that way. He, also, is a victim of *taravana*.

Not the *taravana* of the deep blue yonder. The *taravana* of the cold Modern World.

Tahiti Blues

FRANCESCO

F **RANCESCO** is in love with the South Pacific. Every year he faithfully returns to visit this vast ocean. This voyage is his life's motivation. His yearly pilgrimage.

Francesco is a druggist in Milano, Italy. All year long he saves for this trip. Every box of aspirin sold, every bottle of syrup, every prescription filled adds another mile to the voyage.

Francesco lives his passion in the South Seas : women. All kinds of women. Brunettes. Blondes. Polynesians. Chinese. Philippinos. Indonesians.

But not just any kind of woman. Francesco looks for two essential qualities : the woman must have class, real class. And she must be difficult to conquer. It must seem almost impossible to seduce her. The more inaccessible the lady appears to be, the more exciting she will be to Francesco.

His labors will then start. He will pursue her untiringly, without respite. Expenses will not matter. The lady who catches his fancy will become a real obsession. He will pay court to his prey with passion. Nothing will discourage him. Nothing but an outright refusal. Or vulgar behavior.

Please do not believe Francesco to be coarse or dirty minded. Quite the contrary. It would be rather difficult to find a more civilized man. One could describe him as the end product of an old declining civilization. His obsession with the impossible may be a sign of decadence.

And when his prey finally surrenders, the physical intercourse will have its importance. But the real pleasure for Francesco will come from the surrender of the lady, not the carnal act.

Francesco is what one calls a good looking man. He appears to be much younger than his forty years. His hair is jet black, almost like a gypsy. He speaks four languages fluently. He is well read in Latin and English literature. He is also an inexhaustible source of anecdotes, acquired during his many travels.

His passion for women obliged him to take good care of his body. Thus he still appears to be a young and supple man, and one must get real close to notice a few pronounced facial lines.

Francesco is a true romantic. This is why he loves the South Pacific. What could be more appealing than seducing a beautiful woman on a white sand beach next to a turquoise lagoon?

How sad the colors of the Mediterranean Sea seem after one has been dazzled by the blues of the Pacific. And how romantic it is to walk hand in hand in the softness of the trade winds on a deserted beach.

But Francesco also had a more tactical reason to do his hunting at the antipodes.

To be appreciated, one must be a rare bird. Europe and the Americas are crawling with Italians. But in the South Sea islands, you have to look real hard to find even one of these Latin males.

Francesco considers the South Pacific his private hunting grounds.

He spotted her the first time at Aggie Grey's, the well known hotel of Apia, in Western Samoa. She was eating her breakfast next to the pool.

She was dressed all in white. A white scarf kept her chestnut hair out of her face. Her white calico dress was just transparent enough to reveal well rounded shapes. Even her slippers were white.

All this white was a wonderful contrast to the tropical dark greens of the many plants on the terrace.

She was sipping coffee while listening to the man who sat across the table talking to her with vehemence.

Francesco sat down at the adjacent table. It was not a morning worth celebrating.

The jazzy looking doctor lady from Manila, whom he had pursued and courted since Noumea, via Auckland and Fiji, had turned into a total flop. Just as he was getting set for the final charge, she told him clearly and dryly that she liked him very much and that he had indeed aroused certain feelings. But she was also Filipino and Catholic, and any carnal pleasures had to be irrevocably preceded by a ceremony involving a priest of the Holy Church.

A total disaster indeed. A real Armageddon.

The lady in white and her escort were talking in German. Arguing would be more accurate. The man was having a jealous fit. Francesco listened carefully. This was starting to get interesting. Maybe this year's trip could be salvaged after all.

Thus, he decided to take a real good look at the lady in white. Maybe a prospective prey. His expert eye appraised this new game.

She wasn't quite as young as she would have liked one to believe. But she was surely an exceptional woman.

Some women are cherished by men for their youth and beauty. As time passes, maybe slowly but relentlessly, some of these women, very few, manage to maintain an illusion of youth and freshness. But this takes endless efforts and an iron discipline to achieve.

These ladies are then admired and coveted for this fragile state of conservation. Like high quality preserving.

A famous Paris fashion lady, Coco Chanel, had the right words to describe feminine evolution :

"When a women is twenty years old, she has the face nature has given her. When she reaches forty, she has the face life has shaped. At age fifty, she wears the bloody face she deserves."

The lady in white had a most pleasant face. Still looking young and fresh. A few lines were beginning to appear, but they were the good lines, the lines of happiness. Her body was still superb. Especially her bustline. The light dress showed the lack of a bra, but her breasts were nice and firm and still pointing upward.

As he watched her, Francesco began to get excited. He observed the way she was moving herself. The elegance and smoothness of her gestures. The way she crossed her legs. Her subtle movements when she flicked her cigarette. All real classy.

The Manila doctor lady was already fading rapidly into the past.

The German man was still raving. The lady in white remained impassive. She puffed her cigarette, ignoring him. He got up. Threw his napkin on the table and walked away. Furious. The lady in white sat motionless.

Francesco waited ten minutes. Then he moved over and sat down across from the lady in white.

I shall not reveal here any details on the art of persuasion and seduction of this dear Francesco.

He would never forgive me if I gave away his methods and secrets of courtship. Let me only assure you that he indeed is a Grand Master in the art of seduction. A true descendant of Don Juan.

And he did manage to persuade the lady in white to abandon her escort, a worn-out lover. He talked her into following him to Aitutaki, in the Cook Islands, and on to Rangiroa, an atoll not far from Tahiti.

She turned out to be exactly the type of lady Francesco loved to seduce— very difficult.

Women of European High Society, and those who like to believe they belong, pass out their favors very reluctantly.

The major labor of the man who courts them is to persuade these ladies, actually reassure would be more precise, that he belongs to the same social class. Or to a superior one. The pretender must submit to a sort of test. Many small criteria, most of them not material, are considered proof of belonging. He must then show that he masters the required measures.

And in no way must the lady's surrender appear to be the result of some weakness. There is much talk of love and of other refined matters in these strange rites of precopulation. But real mutual affection is rarely involved. Only the lady's pride and a subconscious class awareness are decisive factors.

It is precisely in this emotional and social mine field that Francesco is an expert. And as hunting women is his passion, he has the necessary patience.

He had encountered failure with the Filipino lady because he was not intimate with Asian mentality. He had applied Western logic to an Oriental context. The lady was dressed like a European. She talked like a Western woman. But it was only icing on a cake. The core still consisted of a thousand generations of Oriental and insular values. With a sprinkle of Spanish Catholicism. He had been doomed to failure even before beginning.

But with the lady in white, he was treading on home

turf. He knew where he was placing his steps. Slowly but surely. Like aging wine.

After a week of patience, a week of services, a week of investments, a week of manners, Francesco finally saw the light at the end of the tunnel. He knew that the surrender would happen tonight. He was certain.

They had arrived the previous day on Rangiroa. At a hotel built as a magnificent little thatched village set along a white sand beach.

Francesco had to rent two bungalows, just as he had at the other hotels where they had stayed. The lady was touchy about her reputation. Even at the other side of the world, where no one cares who among the visitors sleeps with whom. But it didn't matter to Francesco. Expenses had no incidence. What mattered was the final victory. Tonight. He knew it. She had given the little signals.

The weather was beautiful. The sand warm. The sun shining. He spent all afternoon contemplating the thousands of different shades of blue in the lagoon. He was sunbathing, taking rides in the canoe. He was dreaming about tonight. About the surrender of the lady.

After sunset Francesco went to see the maitre d'. To make all the arrangements for dinner. To make it perfect.

Choice of table. Choice of menu. Choice of wine. Choice of champagne. Choice of waitress. Francesco was a well known guest at the hotel. He visited it every year. He loved the small size of this establishment that blended so well in the surrounding environment.

He picked Lalia as waitress. She had often waited on him. She was happy, relaxed and ever smiling.

And what a beautiful dinner it turned out to be. Everything was perfect. An evening with a full moon. How can one describe the beauty of the spectacle when this ball of light slowly rises, with changing colors that are reflected in the mirror smooth lagoon, and a Tahitian band playing island songs in the background.

These moments alone justified the whole long voyage.

Francesco refilled the champagne glasses. Lalia brought coffee. With her unique and charming Tahitian accent, she asked :

"Did Madame and you have a pleasant dinner?"

"Excellent, Lalia. Excellent. Thank you."

And to give the lady in white one last compliment, Francesco added :

"Lalia, this is Madame. It is her first visit. She is very nice."

"Oh, yes, she seems very nice. And lovely too. You are lucky. She's your mother, isn't she?"

The lady in white turned red. She got up without a word. Disappeared into the night, almost running.

Francesco was ashen. He just sat still, stunned. He was paralyzed. It was over. Disaster. So close to success.

Lalia was intrigued by this sudden silence.

"Are you sick?"

Francesco did not answer.

Lalia left and walked toward another table. Thinking that Francesco was strange tonight. She had taken care of them well. She had been nice. And he wouldn't even answer her. These Italians are sometimes really bizarre.

Thus, it seems like Francesco's trip ended in failure that year.

Well, no. Not quite.

The following day the lady in white, incapable of accepting her age and evidently totally lacking a sense of humor, left the hotel in a whirl.

Francesco, now alone, would tell his story to whomever had time to listen. Which means some older guests and the hotel personnel.

Coconut radio saw to it that Lalia was soon told what booboo she had committed. She laughed about it with the other girls, but inside herself, she felt sorry for Francesco. He had always been kind to her.

That night after work she went to her room to take a shower as usual. But then she went out in the moonlight and slipped into Francesco's bungalow. Without a sound she lifted the mosquito netting and cuddled next to him in bed. He woke up pleasantly surprised.

That night was the first time Francesco intimately met a simple girl. A girl without hang-ups. Without complications. Without prejudices.

It was also the first time that he made love for the pleasure of it, not for the conquest. That night he discovered a new dimension, a different taste of things.

He extended his stay another week. He took his time to appreciate the simplicity, the happiness and the laughter of this girl. Every day with Lalia was a day discovering another world. A nicer world. A softer, happier world.

On the day of his departure he went to settle his bill at the reception, smiling.

He did not even take a look at the tall redhead standing next to him, wearing a classy Givenchy sweater. A lady with long, superbly shaped legs. And all the assured movements of high class breeding.

But she had spotted Francesco right away. She had recognized in him a man of distinction. A potential actor to play a role in another amorous 'Grande Complication', one of those complex mating games that are described in the classics. He seemed quite easy to handle. She could make the play last...

But Francesco did not even see her. Or did not want to see her. He just wasn't interested anymore. He had crossed the airlock into a world more simple. More honest. More thoughtful. Much more human.

He walked toward the taxi.

Lalia and her girlfriends were waiting for him there with shell necklaces to kiss him good-bye.

An Outstanding Pearl

PENRHYN. Tongareva in Maori language. Another atoll. Lost in the blue vastness of the Pacific Ocean.

A ring of coral ten miles in diameter. Capped with millions of coconut trees, iron wood trees, screw pines and *miki-miki,* this strange bush that can grow in almost pure sea water.

A huge lagoon. Thousands of shades of blue. A lagoon famous for the quality of its pearls.

Some eight hundred Polynesians live on this barely emerged ring of land. On this fragile environment.

Try to imagine : Stand on the highest point of the island. A little pile of gray coral chunks facing the breakers of an endless swell curling on the barrier reef.

Now look to your right. Only ocean. Five thousand miles of open waters to the shores of South America.

Look to your left. Four thousand miles of rolling swell to Australia. Look behind you. Three thousand miles of sea till the icebergs of Antarctica.

Look in front of you. Six thousand uninterrupted miles to the Bering Straights, frozen ends of Alaska and Siberia.

You just learned what isolation, real isolation, means.

Now lower your eyes. Look well at these poor chunks of coral under your feet. You suddenly shudder. You just realized that they are only ten feet above sea level. The ocean put the coral there. It can take it away just as easily.

A major cyclone. A big earthquake in Chile, Alaska or Japan. An underwater volcanic eruption. A meteorite falling into the sea. Any of these can generate a swell that would just roll over this pile of sand without noticing. And carry everything away. Everything.

In one hour or in one hundred thousand years.

It happened in 1902 to a neighboring atoll. Not a single survivor.

Who then dares say that guys like me who escape to islands are cowards running from reality ?

This must be one of the most dangerous spots on earth. Living here is like playing continuous Russian roulette.

But isn't risk the spice of life?

I spent the night hove-to. It was a calm, moonless night.

I knew that the atoll was about fifteen miles to windward. You can trust the stars and the sun for navigation. But I was also cheating a bit. I had seen the sea birds fly that way at dusk.

You can't see an atoll from far away. The highest coconut trees are about sixty feet tall. Six or seven miles. If your eyes are good.

At five in the morning, I set the jib and mizzen, pulled all sheets tight and locked the tiller.

The coconut trees appeared on the horizon with sunrise, just as I was coming back on deck with a fresh cup of coffee.

An hour later, the pass showed up on the starboard side. Four small crafts were already waiting for me. They had spotted the sails shining in the morning sun. My visit was an event. A change of routine.

The Rarotonga schooner calls only about twice a year. And then only if there is enough copra on the docks of the three Northern Group Islands—Manihiki, Rakahanga, and Penrhyn—to justify the voyage. If three yachts visit, it's a good year.

The island chief came aboard to pilot me through the pass and the coral studded channel to the little village of Omaka. It was easy as it was flood tide.

The whole population stood on the dock to take a look at the newcomer. Especially the vahine, the other boats having already announced the arrival of a single-handed sailor.

While we tied the boat to the pier, a tall bare-chested man wearing an official cap walked toward us. His right arm was missing. He made the following speech :

- "The law of the Cook Islands forbids any vessel to call at Tongareva (Penrhyn in Maori) unless he has cleared first in Rarotonga. But in case of emergency, we may make exception. Rarotonga is far, nine hundred miles away. If we send you there to get a clearance, you shall never come back. We see that you are alone. You have no vahine. This is what we call a real emergency. Thus you may stay. Welcome. Let's celebrate... do you have anything to drink?"

I always keep a case of rum in the bilges for this kind of emergency.

A week was necessary for me to blend into the island community.

Like on many isolated islands, there is a surplus of women. Many young men leave for the big cities of New Zealand and Australia. Few return.

A small group of *vahine* had set up camp next to the boat. Not too close, but close enough not to miss a single movement on the boat. They had stretched out a *peue,* a woven pandanus mat, under the breadfruit tree across from the dock. They giggled with one hand in front of their mouth, one of the typically Polynesian gestures, and were weaving the beautiful hats that gave the atoll a Pacific wide reputation.

I was too far to hear their talk, but knowing them well, I was well aware that these ladies were evaluating me thoroughly. Very thoroughly.

Their long black hair was held back with shiny metal combs. On other islands, the girls have tortoise shell or plastic combs. But here on Penrhyn, a Liberator airplane crashed while landing during World War II. It is still laying at the end of the runway, on the lagoon beach, its torn off engines strewn in a coconut grove. The natives quickly found many uses for the aluminum of the wings and the fuselage.

Several times a day, small groups of ladies would approach the boat and shyly ask to visit below. My vessel had become very popular. The door to the head was covered with a tall mirror. The people living on this atoll had never seen such a mirror. It was the first time its inhabitants could see themselves from head to toe. Some ladies gasped discovering themselves. I quickly left them alone because I felt like a voyeur.

A family adopted me. Old Williams and his two daughters. Still today I feel obliged to this beautiful family for its many kindnesses. I had most of my meals with them, the men first, served by the women. According to old Polynesian custom. The way it should be.

Tioni (John in Maori), the island paramedic, quickly befriended me. He offered to store my beer. The kerosene refrigerator in the infirmary was the only one on the atoll. The penicillin and other medication were crowded a bit to make space for the bottles. In exchange, he solicited games of chess.

It was during these endless games that he told me the island stories that relate the essence of these micro-societies based on oral memories.

He also explained how the constable lost his arm, after I inquired what type of shark had inflicted such damage.

- "It was no shark," he exclaimed. "Our policeman is called Manu. He is the oldest son of the family who lives in the white house next to the church.

"After he had finished his schooling with excellent marks, the family decided to send him to New Zealand. To seek a job. To find a future.

"To save enough money to pay for such a passage takes years. Tons of copra. Hundreds of hats. Tons of mother-of-pearl shells. But all the family united to collect the funds, and Manu left us at age nineteen for the city lights, on the *Manuvai,* the Rarotonga schooner.

"Everyone, of course, was on the dock to wave him away, tears flowing. Success is rare. Returns even more so.

"Several months and several boats later, Manu arrives in Auckland and moves in with an uncle, which is normal for Polynesians whose culture is based on community ties.

"He managed to find a job a few weeks later. In an automobile spare parts plant. In the galvanizing shop.

"The foreman explains the work to him : 'Take the parts brought on this cart with these big pliers. Dip the part one minute in the big barrel in front of you. Then place the dripping part on the cart on your right. That's all. It is simple'.

"Manu does his work carefully all day. He is happy. Happy to know that he has an income. To help his family. To permit them to buy the little things that make the difference between living and surviving.

"In the evening, just before shift change, Manu has a moment of inattention. He lets one part slip into the barrel. He leans over to retrieve it. It burns his arm but he must find the lost part. He searches and searches but cannot feel it. He stands up and looks at his arm. It is gone. Dissolved by the caustic soda. All the other workers explode with laughter."

A shudder runs down my spine. This is not the first time I heard such a story.

How could a young man who grew up on an island, where the most corrosive element is lime juice, ever imagine such horrors as acids, gases or other chemical monstrosities?

- "He must be quite bitter toward the white man?"

- "No. No. He spent a few months in the hospital, then came back home with one arm less. But with a small pension. The joy of everybody was boundless. He had returned. He was back. That was important. The missing arm has no importance. And the tiny pension is very much here, where there is so little. He is a happy man now. Has a beautiful family. He is respected....

"But the most important is that he returned. He didn't get absorbed by the grayness of worker suburbs of the big city. He didn't have time to loose his smile, his joy, his pride, his respect for his fellow, his community sense. He did not have time to be stained by the egoism of consumer society... He is our survivor. We're proud of him...

The medic was also a wise man.

After having been trounced several times in chess, I offered to repair the infirmary water pump. I was feeling sorry for the old man who spent every morning working the old hand pump to move a couple hundred gallons to the roof tank.

A close look revealed that the leather cups of the antiquity had been worn away years ago.

My aft cabin, a complete work shop, contained sheets of leather that I use to reline the gaff jaws. It took less than two hours to shape two beautiful pump cups and install them.

The old man will never forgive me for it. He had always been paid four hours of work a day. Now he gets paid only for an hour every other day.

But the news traveled around the island. The bachelor is also a mechanic. I was solicited by everyone to repair stowed away things. Hand operated sewing machines, some of them the old, old models with spindles instead of bobbins. Equally antique outboard engines.

And strangely enough, many coo-coo clocks.

Yes, you read right; the Swiss chalet type clock with a little bird that comes out to sing coo-coo, coo-coo and then slams the door shut. Surely the last thing one would expect to find on an island lost in the middle of the Pacific Ocean.

These timepieces were brought to Penrhyn by Korean fishing boats that stop in the islands to trade for pearls. A careful examination revealed that they were made in Korea and all had some defect: missing teeth on gear, bent movement, cracked housing, misaligned frame.

Thus, our Korean fishermen bought these defective clocks at some obscure sweatshop, paying about one dollar. But traded them for real, natural, high quality pearls, worth thousands. Here was business more lucrative than fishing. I advised the one-armed constable.

The whole atoll was busy. The Queen's (British, of course) birthday was soon due. The school master asked to borrow my American yacht ensign. He needed it for the festivities.

What a grand celebration it was. The Queen should have been present.

The festivities started with a religious service. Like in all small islands, everyone was in church. The older woman were singing *ute*, shrill songs that are so highly pitched that the women must cover their ears against the pain. Small children were crawling in the center aisle, climbing over two sleeping dogs. All women were dressed in white with beautiful hats. And the singing! Unique. So melodious. So special. You somehow feel closer to God when you listen to these songs.

The religious service ended with a fervent, 'God Save the Queen', and everybody went to a large grassy area next to the lagoon shore on the other side of the village.

Sitting on *peues*, we waited for the show. Not long. Children appeared dressed in more, grass skirts, and started dancing a frenzied *tamure* to the beat of drums accompanied by the laughter of the parents.

It was a quality show. Amazing for such a small community on such an isolated small island.

The population was closely observing my every reaction. Being the only foreign spectator, I represented the whole outside world. I took pain to applaud and laugh loudly and profusely.

After the various dances and singing, four groups of young boys entered the lawn. The first carrying a Union Jack, the British flag. The second, my American yacht ensign. The third, a red flag, Russia, of course. The last held a big Swastika, Germany, for sure.

These four 'countries' simulated Maori combats with long ironwood sticks and spears. The games appeared and were indeed real dangerous, but the art and control of the boys were astounding. The battles proceeded without injuries and the crowd went wild with applause. The British team was declared the winner, of course, out of respect to Her Majesty the Queen.

The celebrations were concluded with a *kai-kai,* a huge feast prepared over several days by the whole population. Two pigs had been slaughtered for the occasion. The crowd was enjoying itself. Rare were the opportunities one had to eat meat.

I walked over to the school master.

"There is a small mistake with your German flag...

"Yes, what is?

"That flag is Hitler's flag. A Swastika. He's dead. The flag has been changed...

He listened patiently to me. Then he got up. Obviously hurt. He returned with a school manual in his hand. Sat next to me and showed me a beautiful full color Nazi flag on a page with "Germany" written underneath. I took the book and leafed through it. It was dated 1938.

It was written. Like the Bible. I only had words. Neither the population, nor the teachers ever heard of Hitler. War, for them, had been a few American Seabees cutting a landing strip with a bulldozer. A dozen planes landing and taking off. And one of them crashing, but no one died. The big event. All beautiful new things. All breaks in the routine. Good for them. Let them keep their vision of the world. It is certainly better than ours.

I apologized :

- "Yes, you must be right. The Swastika is correct. I must have confused it with another country. My apologies...

The schoolmaster was smiling again. That was important.

A few days later, a large fishing vessel entered the pass full steam. He tied up astern of my boat. It was a Korean tuna long liner. The *Dandai Lee Nr 127* hailing from Pusan.

Had we met at sea, I would have smelled him before seeing him, like a sperm whale. A horrible smell drifted from this pile of rust, ropes, glass and plastic floats, drying laundry, strung out shark fins, and a huge pile of fishing nets. The ship looked just as bad as it smelled.

Skinny creatures succeeded in moving around in this maze of equipment and filth. The men wore only underwear, as the interior of this vessel designed for colder climates must have been like a baking oven under the tropical sun. They were just as dirty as their vessel.

On the dock the constable was yelling his little speech, forbidding access to the island. No one listened. Certainly not the captain walking down the gangplank.

This speech was actually only a formality to satisfy the Rarotonga law. Our policeman himself was holding a small jar full of pearls in one hand.

From all huts people were arriving, carrying pearls or hats.

A table and two chairs were brought to the dock for the captain to conduct business on. He was a small Korean, totally bald and so fat he seemed almost round. Tiny short legs managed to carry all that. Every move made him sweat. And smell even worse.

He sat on a chair. The population, one at the time, started showing him the pearls they were willing to trade. In exchange of food supplies, fishing gear or sundries.

After carefully looking at the pearls spread on a plate in the middle of the table, he would grunt like a boar and it would be the turn for the next one.

Most of the pearls displayed were of the *pipi* type, a white pearl with a golden shine, found in small shells very abundant in the lagoon. Some black pearls, growing in large gray shells, would be shown once in a while. Most of them small or 'baroque', that is out of round. There was no pearl farm on the atoll; thus all the pearls were natural and of high value.

It was fascinating to watch the psychological game the captain played. He treated the Polynesians with arrogance. Faked not being interested in the merchandise displayed. He let them wait. Laughed at the pearls shown to him, as if they were valueless. He knew very well time was on his side. He could see that the natives looked with envy at the bags of rice and cases of bully beef that were being slowly stacked next to the table by crew members. The captain knew well that these supplies would be a sought after break in the monotony of a diet based mostly on breadfruit, coconut, a few bananas and fish.

The last islander to show his wares was a distinguished gray-haired man. Tall, slim, in snow-white shorts, he was the total opposite of the captain.

In his hands was a large mother-of-pearl shell. He set it carefully in front of the captain. The slanted eyes of the Asian became almost round. He leaned forward, even stood up to see better. There was cotton in the shell. On this cotton lay a beautiful, exquisite pearl. A real exceptional black pearl. At least sixteen millimeters in diameter. Of grayish color, almost metallic, with blue and green reflections. The round perfect. The image would reflect as clearly as in a fish lens mirror, proof of the natural pearl.

This shell held a unique magnificent pearl. A real jewel. A treasure.

The captain was red all over now. His brain was being overheated by the calculations of the potential profits.

He yelled an order at the ship. A tall skinny sailor came running with a Japanese whisky bottle. The captain tore it from his hands and slammed it on the table. Then he made a gesture for the Polynesian to sit.

The bargaining started as the night was settling in. The women arrived with kerosene lamps, stretched the *peues* close to the table and everybody—men, children and dogs—sat down silently. To observe everything. To miss nothing. To witness this new chapter of the history of the atoll.

The captain was continuously pouring large shots of whisky. The bottle was getting empty. A radio cassette had been added to the pile of goods. The captain was rolling the pearl in the cotton with his fat finger. Inspecting it with his glasses brought by the sailor. But every time he wanted to pick it up, the Polynesian would slap his hand.

- "Buy first. Then you can take it...

And the bargaining went on. The whisky kept flowing. Half way into the second bottle. The sailor even brought five coo-coo clocks, which sent everybody roaring with laughter. As the pile was growing a violent arguing started between the crew and the captain. He was bartering all the ship's supplies. A big yell and the promise to sail straight for Papeete to re-supply restored order.

At four in the morning, just as the Orion constellation was rising in the East, the deal was struck : Fifteen bags of rice. The radio cassette. One drum of vegetable oil. Six bags of sugar. Six cases of corned beef. One drum of kerosene. One case of soy sauce. Two cases of canned lychees. Two bags of onions. Eight bags of flour. One case of whisky. And three rolls of printed cloth.

The fishing boat left the dock at dawn. Everyone went to sleep.

I woke in the evening. The village was busy again. A long table had been placed under the trees next to the church. Girls were decorating it with coconut fronds.

The medic explained :

- "We're having a big feast to celebrate the sale of the pearl. You are also invited. Bring a couple bottles...

- "But all that food will be used up...

- "So what? We are a community. The pearl kind of belonged to everyone. To you too, you're an American... He looked at me with a cunning smile and left, laughing.

It was a real big feast. But made with imported food. Big plates of fried rice. Poe prepared with sugar and bananas. Bully beef fried with onions. The whisky and rum flowing. Lychees for the children. Music from the radio. Billions of stars overhead. Everyone happy and laughing.

A real orgy on an atoll. Soon guitars and drums appeared. The songs and dances became quicker, the gestures more daring. A *bringue* as they say in Tahiti. All night long till dawn.

It took two days to get rid of the hangover. Two peaceful days.

But a woman was always watching me. From a distance. If I turned around, she would stop and smile. If I went on the yacht, she'd sit in the distance and stare my way. She was my shadow.

A little annoyed, I consulted the medic.

- "Why does this woman always follow me?

- "Because she wants you. She likes you...

- "I don't mind, but she's at least forty. That's a bit old for me...

- "She is not forty years old. That's Stella. She must be twenty four. You see, girls age awfully fast on atolls. It's because of the lack of vitamins. Especially vitamin C.

The few reserves they could have accumulated are totally used up with the first birth and nursing. Nursing that lasts up to five years. A baby is the threshold between a beautiful young vahine and an older woman...

"But couldn't the government send vitamin pills?

"Yes, it could. But instead, they send a case of oranges on the schooner at every voyage. Thirty oranges every six months for eight hundred souls. We give them to the babies. You see, we're far away. And quickly forgotten...

"Poor girls!

"Yes. And they know it too. That's why they want to leave the atoll. Before it's too late. That's why Stella follows you...

Back on the boat, I called Stella over. Told her to get aboard. She sat on the cabin roof while I was emptying my ship's pharmacy trying to find every vitamin carried aboard. I also promised her a passage to Rarotonga if she got permission from her family.

Just after I sent her running home, the Korean fishing boat, the one who had bought the pearl, entered the pass full steam ahead.

A few minutes later, she was along the pier, almost tearing my mizzen boom off.

Manu, the constable, came running to deliver his speech. He didn't have time. The captain had already jumped on the dock and now grabbed him by the throat.

"Where is the man who sold me the pearl? Where is he? I want to see him! I want to kill him!

Other men had arrived and were trying to separate the two. The captain was screaming like a pig you bring to slaughter. The Korean sailors were hiding behind their junk. Terrified. They must have endured hell on board.

We had to bind the captain to get him to quiet down.

He then yelled something in Korean. A sailor brought a small carved sandalwood box.

The constable opened it carefully. The cotton was inside. The pearl laying on top.

It had rusted.

Someone on Penrhyn had taken apart the main ball-bearing from one of the engines of the B-24 Liberator plane that had crashed at the end of the runway.

The high quality oil seal had kept the bearing balls like new more than fifty years.

Tahiti Blues

ISLAND SORROW

THE OLD MAN was sitting on the porch. He was sad. He was thinking about the past. His past. These past seventy years. His life.

Sometimes he felt ashamed. So much ashamed that he would cry. When the memories came back. Memories of forty years ago.

How beautiful were the islands then. How easy was life. How nice it used to be to walk along the beach and to greet everyone.

How beautiful was the lagoon. Filled with the colors of coral. The shadows of frightened fish. The clear blue waters.

A few minutes had been all it took to catch the three fish his grandmother needed for lunch.

When he grew up, he went to school, where they taught him that fish keeps better in a freezer than in the lagoon.

He started catching twenty fish a day to buy a freezer, to better keep the fish. When he had bought the freezer, he had to fill it. So, he caught more fish. And to pay for the electricity to keep all this fish he had to catch many more. And to sell all this fish you had to have a car. And to pay for the car he had to catch hundreds of fish every day. But to catch that many fish you needed a motorboat. And to pay for the motorboat you had to catch even more fish, and the lobsters, and the clams, and the tortoises. Everything there was in the lagoon.

This is why the old man cries on his porch today. He cries his shame. Because since a long time ago, there are no more fish in the lagoon. No more lobsters. No more clams. Nothing is left in the lagoon. He cannot even find a fish a day to eat.

He does not cry because he is hungry; he cries because he is ashamed.

Ashamed thinking of his ancestors. They who had thought of him. They who had only taken the necessary. They who had left him a lagoon full of fish. To permit him to feed his children and grandchildren.

He was so ashamed. Because he alone had taken it all just for himself. Like an egoist. Without a thought for others.

He had taken it all to buy those things. Those things they told him were necessary. So that he would be a real man with all these things.

He had believed them. He had cleaned out the lagoon to buy these things. These things that were all broken or rotten since long ago. Lying there in the mud behind the house. But the lagoon is still so empty and dead.

He was ashamed because his children had to leave. They had to go to a big cold city. To work there in a gray and dirty factory. To earn money to buy food. Because here at home, next to their family, there is no more food. There are no more fish. Nothing is left in the lagoon.

This is why the old man is ashamed, sitting there alone on his porch, in front of the empty lagoon. Ashamed to have destroyed alone what a hundred generations had protected before him, to make sure he could feed himself and his children.

He was ashamed to have lived.

Tahiti Blues

A Subject of
Her Majesty the Queen

GOD—or is it nature—does things quite well. The genius of the Creator is sometimes quite amazing. It becomes very apparent if one takes the necessary distance and time to analyze the subject.

We all have the same organs, which all have the same functions. But every human being is unique indeed.

And sometimes, the Creator plays some tricks and offers exceptional beings to us.

Geniuses with incredible intelligence. Women of exceptional beauty.

Others may possess a strong magnetism, an unexplained power that calls for immediate respect.

We have a few individuals with such magnetism in Tahiti : one is a phony Polish baron; the other an Englishman named Alistair.

Alistair was born some fifty years ago, the seventh child of a Liverpool textile mill worker. Beside his life, Alistair's parents could not give him much else. In those days, misery was the common lot of the Midlands working class.

Maybe it was the gloominess that surrounded his youth. Maybe it was the fall he made off that wall at age eleven. Nobody will ever know, but Alistair had abandoned any sense of ambition very early in life.

The only effort Alistair ever thoroughly pursued in his life was to master a perfect imitation of the symbol of British class rigidity, the 'Oxford accent'.

This accent, added to his unique magnetism, a dignified way of walking, and a shyness that could be perceived as arrogance, gave Alistair the appearance of a man of the world. Proud, assured, and used to all worldly pleasures. Luxuries he had rarely, if ever, tasted.

I do not know how he landed on our distant shores. Some tell the story of a furious captain firing an incompetent sailor. But I'm sure it is only stupid gossip. And who cares anyhow?

My first encounter with Alistair goes back a few years, on the island of Bora-Bora.

That day, an accomplished gentleman checked into my small hotel. He was followed by a bearded Hindu of medium height who was wearing thick glasses. The gentleman booked two bungalows. I was most impressed to have the honor to accommodate such a distinguished guest.

I showed the Hindu where to take the gentleman's luggage. He did seem a bit reluctant at first, but on my insistence, he executed the order. Thus I was able to pursue my conversation with this most select customer. You must understand that he was my first client with a servant. Such a rare sight these days. A whiff of the good old days.

That evening, at dinner, I asked the gentleman if I might join them for coffee. The Hindu answered that I might.

The minutes that followed made me realize the enormity of my mistake. The Hindu was the director of a bank in Papeete. It was he who had hired Alistair as guide for a business trip to the Leeward Islands. Because he had felt sorry for the financial plight of the Englishman. Maybe also in memory of a former great Empire.

The hazards of life had made their ways cross. Ramesh, the Hindu, had found Alistair at the end of a small valley west of Papeete.

A flat tire on a muddy road, close to a miserable plywood shack. A man comes from the shack to help change the wheel. They soon realize they both speak English. Alistair introduces Ramesh to his wife and four children. They drink tea sitting on the old automobile seat that is the house sofa. And since that day, every time Ramesh needs help, he calls on Alistair.

But, back to our story on Bora-Bora. I had indeed made the big goof of reversing the roles. I profusely apologized to Ramesh. But, thank God, he is an intelligent man with a great sense of humor and without hang-ups. This incident actually made very good friends out of us, and we still laugh today about this mix-up.

I opened a few bottles of my best wine, which we emptied with no pain. Then I even fetched a few more. The high quality liquor diluted enough of Alistair's timidity to get him to tell us the big adventure of his life. His moment of glory :

One morning, a superb ship enters Papeete harbor on the island of Tahiti. It is the *Britannia*. The private yacht of Her Majesty The Queen, Elizabeth II, Sovereign of Great Britain and what little is left of the British Empire.

The ship had carried Her Gracious Majesty on her official visit to Australia and Papua New Guinea. The Queen had left the yacht in Honiara in the Salomon Islands to board a plane bound for London.

The royal vessel is returning to Plymouth via the Panama Canal.

The Britannia ties up at the visitor's dock downtown. The captain pays a courtesy visit to the French governor. He presents an invitation to a dinner aboard. For His Excellency, his high collaborators and their wives. And also for the subjects of Her Majesty residing in Tahiti. All in the name of the Duke of Wallop, cousin of the Queen and midshipman aboard the yacht. Would His Excellency the Governor please be so kind as to notify these subjects?

The governor gives orders. The 'Sureté' (French secret police) has only two British citizens in their books : the spouse of an automobile importer and Alistair.

The governor's personal driver is dispatched to deliver the superbly engraved invitations hand-written by the Royal Calligrapher. He has a few difficulties finding Alistair's miserable shack at the end of the muddy trail. But, being Tahitian, he thinks nothing of it and hands the envelope to Hina, Alistair's wife.

Alistair reads the invitation with great pleasure. He lovingly fondles the raised engraved coat of arms on the letter. After all these years, the Motherland had not forgotten him.

The invitation calls for Mister and Missus. He explains it to Hina. How important it is to him.

But she refuses to go. She explains that she is old now. That 'her sun has set', as she says. That she has born and breast-fed four children. That she has raised them. That she now prefers to hide.

He decides to take Hortense, his oldest daughter, along. She recently celebrated her nineteenth birthday. She is a beautiful young woman, and, like all Tahitian girls, totally at ease in her skin. She inherited the Polynesian features of her mother and the happiness and femininity of the island girls.

Alistair scrapes all his money together. Just enough to buy Hortense a new pare'u (lava lava, sarong) and pay for a short taxi ride.

He opens the old wooden chest to get his white suit that is wrapped in mothballs. Hina washes it and presses it carefully with the charcoal iron.

On the glorious evening, Hortense and Alistair walk, shoes in hand, the two miles to the main road. There, they rinse the mud off their feet at a faucet and hitchhike to town. Then they hire the best looking cab for the last mile to the dock.

The royal Yacht gleams in the night, its thousand lights ablaze and reflected by the smooth harbor waters. The taxi glides silently along the dock to the companionway lit up by powerful spotlights.

An officer in gala uniform runs to open the door. Hortense gets out of the cab, dazzled. Alistair follows. Seeing this distinguished gentleman accompanied by such a lovely woman, all men stand to attention and remain thus while Hortense and Alistair walk slowly up the gangway.

The duty officer takes a quick look at the invitation :

- "But of course, Sir. We were expecting you. All other guests have arrived."

And he bows deeply to Hortense.

- "My respects, Madame. Please follow me."

They enter the Royal Salon, a huge cabin with wood paneled walls, on which hang portraits of defunct monarchs.

At the center of the room is a long table set with the most beautiful linen and silverware and lit by six large crystal candelabras.

The 'crème de la crème' of the island government and their wives, some Tahitian, chatter in small groups with the officers. They talk, holding champagne glasses. The ladies wear beautiful dresses, but Hortense, with her blue *pare'u* tied over the shoulder and her crown of gardenia flowers over her long black hair, does not look out of place. Quite the contrary. Simplicity is very often the ultimate elegance.

The officer introduces them to the host. He is Lord Wallop, Duke of Upper Wallop and a close cousin of Her Majesty. He is a pleasant young man in a white midshipman uniform, with a face full of freckles. Hortense manages very well the reverence her father taught her that afternoon.

A steward offers champagne. The duty officer sticks to Alistair. He is puzzled by the exceptional personality of this gentleman in the company of such an exotic beauty. He engages in conversation :
- "Hum...Sir... Looking at you walk, I dare say you used to be in Her Majesty's armed forces... hum...hum..."
- "Quite right, Lieutenant, quite right."

Alistair does not say more. An intelligent man, he learned a long time ago that silence can be much more impressive than talk. If you explain your life, it is bound to appear quite common. But if you keep silent, it will take on the dimensions that the imagination of the other person is prepared to give it. Which sometimes can be boundless.

And the officer pursuing him is the perfect product of these so-called 'Public Schools', the fancy private schools from another century. Proper education, impeccable manners and a strong ego would forbid him to ask a straight question. It would be a 'lack of manners' indeed. He starts again :
- "Hum... hum... I'd place you... yes...in the Scottish Highlanders, captain, maybe..... Wouldn't I recognize a very slight Scotch accent?"

- "Not quite, not quite, Lieutenant."

Alistair let his eyes sweep the salon. He finds Hortense standing next to Queen Victoria's portrait, already surrounded by three midshipmen, caring for all her needs.

The lieutenant goes on :

- "Hum...But, of course. How stupid of me...It's obvious... Royal Air Force...isn't it?"

- "Not quite, Lieutenant, not quite."

- "Hum...hum... I see. Yes, yes...you used to be in B.I.C. (Burma, India, China.)"

- "Not quite, Lieutenant, not quite."

- "Hum...hmmm...of course.... But I know you were not Navy...."

- "Quite correct, Lieutenant, I did not have the pleasure to serve in the Royal Navy."

The officer iss more and more puzzled. He remains silent.

The captain of the Britannia is now coming toward them and asked to be introduced to Alistair :

"- Delighted, Sir, really delighted... to see Old Britannia so well represented in these far islands... Just between us... we've got to show these Frenchies what class... I mean real class, is... haven't we...?"

He takes a long look toward Hortense, leans slightly over toward Alistair and pursues :

- "...This is really quite a stunning specimen of native lady you have brought along there... beautiful indeed... It does show your impeccable taste... my congratulations, indeed... I see that the harsh tropical life does have a few compensations... hum... If I may say so... excuse my frankness, Sir... but we are among gentlemen, aren't we?"

He giggles, "I must admit that I do sometimes envy expatriates the likes of you... And when your mission will be accomplished, you shall spend peaceful days in some Kent manor... won't you... but all these memories will be with you... Oh, do I envy men the like of you... It's been a great pleasure, I can assure you...Yes, yes... please keep up the excellent work... You do represent us so well... yes, indeed... Well, Sir, I hope to have the honor of chatting with you again...yes.. .Good bye, Sir...."

And he leaves, taking the lieutenant aside and whispering to him :

- "You personally will take care of this guest, will you ?"

The officer returns with a new glass of champagne for Alistair :

- "Hum... hum... A great man, a fine chap, our captain... well bred, isn't he ? His uncle is Lord Fincham... hum...."

- "But of course. A great man. An excellent observer. Amazing indeed!"

Encouraged by the captain's words, the officer pursues his inquiry :

- "Hum...Sir. Aren't you our consul on Tahiti...?"

- "Not quite, Lieutenant, there is no British consul presently in French Polynesia."

- "Hum... hum... But of course... Oh yes, of course... I see... Hum... Weren't you in the Commandos, our Special Forces, Sir...?"
- "Not quite Lieutenant, not quite."

Alistair sips his champagne with delight while observing his surroundings.

The officer scratches his head. He is confronted with a most unusual case. He takes great pride is his ability to place all people in society. He has refined this capacity to an art. It is of vital importance for him to discover this man's secret. This gentleman is a tough case. He must succeed or his reputation of social profiler will be in jeopardy.

Everyone is now sitting down for dinner. The host, the Duke of Wallop, proposes a toast to Her Majesty the queen and the President of the French Republic. Everyone raises a glass.

Alistair is seated between the wife of a government counselor and the lieutenant. The officer is not able to further question his neighbor because Alistair is continuously solicited by the other guests to translate.

It is only at the end of the sumptuous meal, while coffee is being poured and cigars are being passed to the gentlemen, that the lieutenant dares approach Alistair again :

- "Hum, hum... But of course... how stupid of me... hmmm... You were in Army intelligence, weren't you...?"
- "Not quite, Lieutenant, not quite."

The lieutenant turns all red. He doesn't understand anymore. He's mentioned all Armed Forces branches. Almost all. But what could this important man have been doing in the Armed Forces ?

He excuses himself and leaves, thoughtful.

Alistair walks among the other guests and the officers. He listens to conversations here and there, answers greetings and small talk.

He leaves Hortense and her court alone. It is a great pleasure for him to see her evolve in such refined society. Alistair does not worry at all about her. Polynesians have a unique ability to adapt to new surroundings and situations. And an inborn sense for ceremonial, one of the bases of their culture. They always observe all gestures and habits of the surrounding people thoroughly before making a move. Then they make the proper one.

You can take any Polynesian from any isolated village and parachute him into Buckingham Palace. He will seem totally at ease there and make all the right moves. It is this unique adaptability to any ceremonial behavior that so much impressed British and French aristocracy in the late eighteenth century. The pompous classes were so pleasantly surprised by the civility of these natives that they created the myth of the 'noble savage'.

Alistair is continuously solicited to translate for high officials. He does it with grace while sampling with great pleasure the excellent cognac and hearty port wine passed around by the stewards.

It is now past midnight. He blinks his eyes at Hortense. She takes leave from her many escorts.

They thank the host and the captain, and slowly walk down the gangway. On the dock, the lieutenant catches up with them :

- "Hum...hum...Sir. Would you like a taxi ?"

- "No thank you. We were going to enjoy this balmy night a while."

The officer leans toward Alistair and whispers :

- "Hum...hum...Pardon my manners, Sir. But I do think I've got it...Hum...You have my officer's word that your secret is safe. Hum...You must be our local station chief for M.I.6 (British intelligence).

- "Not quite, Lieutenant, not quite."

The officer is frantic now.

-"But then, Sir, what was your branch. Hum...Please pardon my manners, Sir, but I am at a loss. I shall keep your secret; you already have my word...Please Sir...."

- "My dear Lieutenant, I was a bugler. The Call to the Dead was my specialty. Have a pleasant night, Lieutenant."

Hortense and Alistair disappear in the night.

The officer is stunned. He stands motionless, then slowly drifts toward the *Britannia*.

The captain is waiting for him at the top of the gangway :

- "Well, Lieutenant... Amazing gentleman, isn't he ? Real class, I'd say... quite rare indeed... Have you discovered what he does? He does not talk much...not much at all, I'd say."

The lieutenant gets close to the captain and speaks softly :

"- Hum...Yes, Sir, indeed... Hum... And with good reason... hum.... Well, he happens to be our local intelligence agent... hum... I know his secret is safe with you, Sir."

"Beautiful, Lieutenant... beautiful ! I see that you are a very cunning observer indeed... You see, London had notified me personally on confidential matters concerning this gentleman... I must admit I wanted to put your talents to a test... Congratulations, Lieutenant... my sincere congratulations... you are as sharp as ever... I shall mention it in my reports."

The lieutenant almost betrayed his thoughts with a furtive smile.

Hortense and Alistair walked all the way home. It was too late to hitch a ride. They arrived three hours later in front of the little shack, their shoes in their hands. Hina was sitting on the porch, next to the kerosene lamp, waiting for them.

Tahiti Blues

The Ghost of the Palace Hotel

TAKE A WALK at night in the villages and in the countryside of Tahiti. You will see that each house has a dim light that burns all night long in at least one of the rooms. Generally it is a kerosene lamp. No Polynesian would dare sleep without such a light. He would be terrified, have nightmares.

You need such a lamp to keep the *tupapau*, the spirits of the ancestors, the ghosts, at bay.

Ghosts are no laughing matter in Tahiti. They are always around us, still today. Neither automobiles, nor electricity, nor television have succeeded in chasing them away. The spirits are part of the family and everyday life, just like your grandmother.

You must learn to live with them; you must learn to respect them. And they'll leave you in peace. But if you make fun of them, or, even worse, ignore them, they'll make you pay. Sometimes dearly.

*Tupapau*s are everywhere. But they prefer to live in stones. Stone tikis, tombstones and especially *maraes* (ancient ceremonial grounds).

*Marae*s are large platforms built out of rocks or coral slabs. They virtually litter all islands of the Polynesian Triangle. They are the temples of ancient family cults. And human sacrifices. The more human skulls that were displayed on a *marae*, the more respected the family would be.

On Tahiti, you'll find *marae*s anywhere. Thus, you're bound to disturb at least one of them if you want to build something big.

That is what happened during construction of two luxury resorts in the suburbs of Papeete.

The story is almost always identical : the ruins of some *marae* are exactly where the architects have decided to place the building foundations. So you have to dig.

The construction supervisor, just transferred from the States, gives the order to the bulldozer operator :

- "Make a pile with those stones over there!"

- "But, Boss, you're crazy, it's a *marae*!" pleads the Tahitian driver.

A big argument ensues. The operator refuses to disturb any of the stones. He'd rather get fired. The supervisor insists. The hotel has got to be built. He will end up having to drive the dozer himself to remove all 'that pile of stones'.

The Tahitian workers will watch him with big round eyes. They'll feel sorry for the white man. He will have nightmares. He will get sick. He might loose a limb. Or even a loved one may die.

These two hotels have their 'resident ghosts'.

The *tupapau* of the hotel likes to walk around dressed in a white gown. At night.

This hotel has been built along the slope of a hill. To respect the local zoning laws that forbid any buildings to be higher than a coconut tree, they built the resort hugged against the slope of a steep hill. Because of this, the lobby and first floor are at the top, and the twelfth floor is all the way down the hill. Where the *marae* used to be. Where the *tupapau* likes to roam at night.

No employees dare go down to that floor at night. Neither the maids nor the mechanics. Because the elevator machinery is also at that level. Should a motor or control break down, it will not be repaired until the next morning. Tough luck for the guests. They'll have to use the stairs.

The *tupapau* is smart. He likes tourism. He does not want to bother visitors. He will only show himself to employees or natives. But the guests complain : no room service; no maids after dark.

After a few years of listening to unhappy clients, the hotel manager has heard enough. He decides to take care of this problem once and for all. He puts an ad in the newspapers in Switzerland.

"Large Tahiti resort hotel seeks top housekeeper. Applicants must have strong personality, good health and must not believe in ghosts. This is a serious offer with top pay and fringe benefits, etc..."

The manager himself had flown to Europe to choose the right person. She arrived a month later. She was most professional. She had been selected among a couple hundred candidates.

She was a rather heavy set Swiss lady. Her hair was tied into an austere bun. She walked clicking her heels. No smiles. No laughter. It would be analyzed as a sign of weakness. She was a graduate from the Lausanne Hotel School. You could not find anyone more efficient. More strict. More clean. More neat. More *'blitze-blank'*, like they say over there.

She stirred up the girls like a tornado. Commands were flying. She was everywhere. She was never satisfied. The maids were even running at times. The rooms were spotless. The bathrooms shining. The manager was giggling with pleasure.

The second night, she ordered :

"Prepare the beds in the rooms! One team on the twelfth floor!"

Hearing this, the girls stopped dead in their tracks.

No way would they go down there. Everyone refused. Big argument. Screams and fits from the Swiss lady. Tears and stoicism from the maids. Nothing doing. It was a mutiny. The girls would not go.

But the lady would not give in. She would show them. She would prove to these primitive people that ghosts are fairy tales. She would make the beds herself. Once. Then there would be no more excuses. The girls would have to go!

Slamming her heels, she marched to the elevators, bucket in one hand, broom in the other. The maids followed her, begging her not to go, imploring her to reconsider.

She did not bother to answer. Proud, condescending, she entered the elevator and disappeared behind the closing doors.

The girls waited twenty minutes. Terrified. Some were crying, others even praying. They felt sorry for the lady. Even though she was so severe.

The elevator came back to the main floor. The doors opened.

The lady stepped out. Ashen. White like a sheet. Without bucket. Without broom. She walked toward her room. Like a robot. Without a word. She packed her bags. She went to the reception. Hired a cab to the airport. Still ashen. Still without a word.

The manager found her at two o'clock in the morning in the deserted airport hall. Sitting alone on a bench waiting for the next international flight. Her eyes staring straight in front of her. He questioned her. She remained mute. She was like dazed.

She left the island on the next morning plane.

No one ever found out what happened that evening on the twelfth floor.

Still, no one makes beds at night and elevators sometimes do not get repaired before morning.

But another classy hotel, a palace on the west coast, also has its ghost. Its own *tupapau*.

I still remember perfectly the grand opening of that hotel. It was a great day for Tahiti. A big celebration. The inauguration of the first modern international class resort. Totally air conditioned. Glass, mirrors and marble everywhere. A phone in every room. Concrete throughout. Nothing could rot. The population was dazzled. The modern world had reached them. The tourists were less dazzled. They found the same bed, the same chair, the same curtains as in the rooms of the big city hotel they had left the day earlier. Ten thousand miles to discover that the universal "standardizer" had preceded them...

Everyone from Papeete had come. The 'high society' of this provincial town. And all those who thought they belonged. Which means everybody was there. The newspapers and their photographers were also there. So everyone came with the legitimate spouse, not the mistress.

The governor had arrived in gala uniform, all white with gold braided scrambled eggs. He cut the blue, white and red ribbon as the crowd applauded. The military band played the Marseillaise, sweating heavily.

The crowd then stormed to the bar and the buffet. The Tahitian ladies formed little groups to gossip. The European ladies tried to impress each other. The men drank and tried to appear important.

The inauguration is a great success.

From a side door, an employee waves frantically to Romain, the general manager :

"Boss, there is no more water in the hotel!"

"Take care of it! Call the engineer! Call the plumbing contractors, whatever, but get it fixed!"

Throughout the celebration, the water supply is shut off, comes back, shuts off again, comes back again, and so on. Because of this, toilets back up and smell, and a real panic ensues in the kitchens. The manager is fuming. Everything was supposed to have been checked and rechecked.

Toward the end of the inauguration the water supply comes back to normal. And stays that way for the next two weeks.

Everyone on the island heard about the incident. Everyone knew now that the Grand Palace also had a ghost, a *tupapau*. A smart *tupapau*. He had waited for the great celebration to announce it himself. Even though his *marae* had been a tiny one. A miserable little stone slab that very few skulls must have decorated.

But Tahiti started to love this *tupapau*. Everyone loves anecdotes that break the monotony of island life. Especially when they involve expatriates fresh in the Territory. Who descend on us like missionaries. Carrying the message of their society, which they believe to be superior. The best. The perfect system. The only valid one. But they always forget that the populations of the big cities, the cradles of the perfect societies, all dream about small imperfect communities like Tahiti.

Maybe Ancient Polynesia and its *tupapau* could teach something to this foreign and arrogant world. Isn't life in our small islands a never ending lesson of modesty?

The water supply was being interrupted again once in a while. Usually in the morning. Sometimes in the afternoon. Always the same way. Pressure drop, a few minutes no water, then water again. It would keep being shut on and off like that, sometimes during a five minute span, but mostly fifteen minutes long. Rarely more.

Of course, Romain, the manager, calls many meetings with the architects and the plumbing contractors. They inspect the miles of pipes. But everything seems perfect. The cause had to be the supply, that is the government system.

Polite complaint to the authorities. They send their engineers to inspect the reservoirs and the main ducts. Denial from the public authorities. The tanks are full when the hotel supply is interrupted. All the surrounding houses, fed by the same system, have a steady supply. The problem must lie within the resort.

And the water shutoffs keep on happening. But never on weekends.

Everyone then talks about a Christian ghost. A *tupapau* who respects the Sabbath. This is getting more and more interesting.

But Romain does not laugh at all. Guests complain more and more. One even got burned when the hot water suddenly came back on.

He then decides to call headquarters in France.

"Send the best specialists. Right away. I don't give a damn if it costs a mint!"

Tahiti is holding its breath. This was getting more and more interesting.

The specialists arrive two days later on the next plane from Europe. With a ton of X-ray and electronic gear.

During the following two weeks the specialists and their team open ceilings, take valves apart, blow air into pipes, X-ray welds, recheck diagrams, install pressure gauges, test the supply system. To no avail. Everything seems perfect.

Romain calls a meeting and asks to hear the results from the specialists.

- "Sir, we have checked the whole system. From A to Z. Everything is built to specifications and there are no obstructions in the pipes."

"Then how do you explain the water shutoffs?"

"We have no explanation. No technical explanation. Nothing logical. Maybe you really do have a ghost!"

Romain is fulminating. Mad as a dog. He spent millions to hear this nonsense. Ghosts do not exist. He is almost crying.

The Tahitian secretary, who is taking notes, suggests :

"Why not ask the *tahua* of Papara. They say he is the best."

"What the hell is a *tahua*?"

"One of the healers. The ones that cure you with herbs. They know the old customs. The one in Papara is called Tupua. He is the only one who accepts taking care of the big *marae* of Mehetia. The most powerful of all *marae*. He is buddy with the *tupapaus*."

"I need no medicine man. I'm not crazy!"

But the following day, after having heard again a series of clients complaining, Romain tells his secretary :

"Take my car and go tell your wizard to come."

He came the following day. Romain expected to see a tall gray-haired wise man, like in the movies. He was short and fat. Dressed only in a pair of oversized shorts that rural Tahitians love to wear. He had parked his old rusty pick-up right in front of the reception. An old woman wrapped in a *pare'u* (lava-lava) sat in the back.

She gave Romain a big smile, who could thus appreciate her total lack of teeth.

He took the old *tahua* to his office. The man sat in one of the comfortable chairs with pleasure, grinning widely. The secretary came to translate.

Romain explained his dilemma. The old man listened to the translation, then replied

"I know your problem. It is a *tupapau* of the Haerepo, the troubadours of the ancient days. This one died because he drank too much kava. He has been curing his hangover for centuries. You disturbed him by building this house that is too big.

"He is mad at you now. Real mad. Not only did you destroy his home, but now you say he does not exist. You add insult to injury. That is not nice. You are the one who came to bother him. You must ask his forgiveness."

"How ?"

"You must show him your respect. You must believe in him. You must organize a big ceremony. A fire-walk."

"How much will this cost ?"

"Whatever you feel like giving. I do not charge. It's forbidden. If someone asks for money, then he is not a true *tahua*."

Romain had already discussed it with his secretary. She had mentioned that the old man was known to like to down a few.

Coming from a suspicious world, he offered :

"I'll give you four cases of whisky and twenty cases of beer. Half of it now, the other half after success."

The old *tahua* remained silent for a while, than stood up. He said :

"OK. But I see you do not have trust. Be assured. I do not talk if I can not do. Should I not succeed appeasing your *tupapau*, every kid in Tahiti would make fun of me. Would tell me that my *mana*, my power, is like a rotten banana. Just good for the chickens. It would be worse than death. One cannot live without the respect of the community. You gamble a few bottles. I gamble my life. Think about it. And think also about the poor *tupapau*. He has no more home. Forever."

The bellboys were loading the precious merchandise in the jalopy.

The old man gave directions to the hotel employees how to dig the pit for the fire walk. Where to get the stones. Which wood to fetch.

They left the hotel in a cloud of smoke from the sputtering engine, the grandmother stuck between the cases of beer in the back. The hotel employees were cheering them off. This was living proof that the *mana*, the power of the ancient religion was still alive and well.

The *tahua* came every night to the hotel. He would sit next to the huge pit that had been dug, singing monotonous notes in old Tahitian. Or he would remain seated without any movement for hours, like a stone statue. He checked that the wood was properly placed. After the tons of stones had been laid on top, he spent days striking them with leaves of the ti, from a shrub that grows in the mountains.

Everything was soon ready. The ceremony would take place on Friday night.

Romain invited all the hotel guests to assist. Might as well put all this hocus pocus to some use, he thought.

That Friday night, after dark, the *tahua* arrived with a small group of men. Mostly old. All dressed in lava-lavas. Romain recognized a few hotel employees among them.

Luau torches had been set all around the pit. The wood had been lit that morning. Now that it was night the red hot stones glowed in the dark, like a vision from an inferno. A Tahitian drum sounded a monotonous rhythm, like a heart beat. All the hotel guests were present. But also hundreds of people from town. Mostly natives. No one from outside the hotel had been invited. It looked like Coconut Radio had worked wonders again.

The *tahua* and another old man each picked up two branches of ti. They held them like candles. They walked toward the pit.

The drum beat quickened a little. The two old men stepped forward. Barefoot on the glowing rocks. They seemed to be hypnotized. Carefully, they stepped from burning rock to burning rock. The crowd was silent. Mesmerized. Slowly the men reached the opposite end of the pit.

Back on the lawn they walk around the pit, just as slowly. They came toward Romain. He congratulated them. The old man talked.

- "What did he say?", Romain asked his neighbor.

- "Your turn now. Take your shoes off!"

Romain was stunned. Refused to go. The old man explained quietly that it was at him that the spirit was mad. So he must go. Or everything would be useless. If he believes in the ghost, then he would not get burned. And he showed his foot soles. They were untouched.

- "But you must believe in the spirit," concluded the old man.

Romain looked around him. Thousands of eyes were locked on him. Even those of his clients. This was a real trap. He thought about his career. He had to go. There was no possible escape.

He removed his shoes and socks. Slowly, he walked toward the pit. The searing heat surprised him. He took a step backward. But the two old men were on each side of him. They grabbed his arms and pulled him forward. The tahua whispered :

- "You believe spirit!"

Romain tried. Tried to think about the ghost. The old men were holding tight. Moving slowly forward. He felt the heat under his feet. The pain. He wanted to scream. He couldn't. He thought of the ghost. The pain disappeared. The old men were almost carrying him now. Their strength seemed incredible. He almost fainted.

And then it was over. They had reached the other end of the pit. He had done it. His head was spinning. He wanted to faint. But he caught himself.

The crowd was applauding. Suddenly he was surrounded by his staff. Everyone congratulated him. Everyone wanted to shake his hand. Bunch of hypocrites. Where were they when it was time to go ?

The *tahua* came toward Romain and thanked him. Romain invited him for a drink, but he disappeared.

Much later, after quite a few whiskies and having told his feelings several times, Romain looked at his feet that were starting to hurt. They were badly burned. He asked to be driven to the infirmary.

The duty nurse, already well informed about what had happened, received him like a hero. But when she examined the feet, her face got serious :

- "You didn't listen to the *tahua*. You didn't believe in the spirit. Look now. You have second degree burns...

Romain left the dispensary with his feet wrapped in huge bandages protected with plastic bags.

The next day he hardly left his office. He had to walk with crutches. His feet were really hurting now. He was furious. Looking at his heavily bandaged feet wrapped in plastic bags, he thought of being the laughing stock of Papeete. Actually, it was quite the contrary. He was the hero of the day.

The following Monday the water problems happened as usual. Upon hearing this, Romain really threw a fit. He was screaming with fury.

He wanted to grab the tahua and roast his feet with a blowtorch. Or fry them in the big chicken broiler of the main kitchen. He could imagine the laughter at headquarters in Paris. He had been had by a native medicine man. He had given him the key to the bar to have his feet toasted in some stupid savage ceremony. In front of all the guests. His career was shot. He'd end up managing a third rate joint somewhere along some boondocks highway.

At that moment there was a knock on the door. It was the chief engineer and a gardener. All excited :

- "Boss, boss! I found the *tupapau*!"

- "What. You dare talk about ghosts. Look at my feet!"

- "But boss, listen. I found him. True. It is the kids. This morning I came to work late because the motor scooter of my wife's stepmother had a flat tire. When I passed an hour late in front of the hibiscus bushes, the ones next to the main gate, I heard noises. I went to see. There I saw the kids of Mama Iris. They were sitting on the main water duct that supplies our water. They were playing with the big gate valve. Using it like the steering wheel of a truck. Making 'vrummm-vrummm' noises while turning the big wheel. In the morning. While waiting for the school bus. That's how they shut the water off to the hotel. There is no school on weekends, so they don't play."

Romain did not answer. He was only looking at his feet.

The engineer then talked :

- "I put a big chain and padlock on the valve. It can't happen anymore."

The manager kept looking at his feet.

- "Aren't you happy I found the reason, boss?" asked the gardener.

But Romain still didn't answer. He was already preparing the speech he would give to the *tahua*. He was ready to tell him the truth. He was going to hear what he thought about ghosts and fire walks. Just some bloody kids.

The *tahua* showed up on Wednesday, the empty beer cases in the back of the collapsing pick-up. This time there were two old ladies stuck between the cases. They had flower crowns askew on their heads, guitar and ukulele in their hands, and were yelling songs with shrill voices. They seemed to just have finished the last case of beer.

Of course, this wheeled monument to boozing had to park again right in front of the high class reception lobby. The tourists, for sure, saw lots of local color that day.

Romain arrived as fast as possible, limping on his feet wrapped like a mummy. He started yelling and pointing at the *tahua* with his crutch. A bellboy ran up to translate :

- "What do you want here? I should take you to court. Look at my feet!"

- "Your problem is solved. The spirit has forgiven you. I kept my word. I've come to collect the second half of your word."

- "But there was no ghost. The kids did it. Leave right now or I shall call the cops!"

The old man remained silent a few minutes. He did not lose his cool, nor his smile.

- "You do not understand things. It is the *tupapau* that gave a flat tire to Petero's wife's stepmother. That way he would be late. That way he could discover the kids. That way you could put a padlock on the gate valve. A ghost cannot install a padlock, can he?"

- "You really believe me to be a total idiot, don't you ? And that I believe your fairy tales. Leave! You shall get nothing. This place is off limits to you. Go. Or I call the police!"

The old man looked sad. He made a sign to the women to unload the empty cases. He looked at Romain.

- "You are not a just man. You do not keep your word. The spirit will get upset again. Do not ask for my help then."

- "You did me in once. Never again. Ghosts DO NOT exist. Only stupid people believe in them. Get lost.

A bellboy came then running up to Romain.

- "Boss, boss. There is no more electricity in the hotel!"

The manager turned around and looked at the huge glassed reception area. It was completely dark. People were trying to open the electrically operated doors. Some were banging on the glass panels.

In the driveway, the old women were unloading the last cases of empty bottles. The *tahua* started the noisy engine.

Romain turned to the old man. Looked into his eyes, and said :

"Just a minute, sir. Please wait."

Then he called out to the bell boy :

"Put ten cases of beer and two cases of whisky in the gentleman's car!"

The two old ladies gave Romain beautiful toothless smiles. They started their singing again.

And the hundreds of fluorescent lights of the reception began blinking back on...

Tahiti Blues

Deep Metal

IT'S TUESDAY. There is only one client for my hotel aboard the daily plane.

He is a lonely young man, carrying a navy bag.
He checks in and rents an overwater bungalow for a week.

Much too curious as usual, I strike up a conversation.
The young man turns out to be the medical doctor on the oceanographic research vessel that arrived the previous day in Papeete.
The ship is in the South Pacific on a scientific mission studying polymetallic nodules. A bent propeller shaft calls for hauling the ship out at the French Navy yard in

Tahiti. At least two weeks in dry dock. The ship's doctor decides to take this opportunity to visit the island of Bora-Bora.

That evening, we sit on the dock facing the lagoon and watch the sunset fireworks. The girl brings two fresh gin and tonics.

I break the silence:

- "Tell me about nodules."

- "Well, if you're interested."

He takes a long sip from his drink, crunches a few ice cubes, and tells me this strange but true story:

- "We are trying to establish a chart that shows the location of nodule fields. They say the Pacific seabed is littered with nodules. We have found a few major lodes already. Mainly south of Hawaii and west of Clipperton atoll.

A nodule is the accumulation of metal particles. Mostly iron, copper and manganese. Which crystallize around some foreign object that sank to the ocean bottom. It has about the size and shape of an Idaho potato.

They say that millions of tons of these nodules litter the Pacific Ocean floor. All one has to do is pick them up.

"But there lies the difficulty. They are at least two miles deep, most of the time three miles deep.

We collect samples. The stern of the ship is equipped with a monstrous winch that can handle eight miles of steel cables. To pull a steel bucket that scrapes the ocean floor. We generally dredge an hour at a time. Then we might spend eight to twelve hours getting the bucket back to the surface.

"I'm also in charge of all photography on board. As the sixteen man crew hardly ever gets sick or wounded, it helps me keep busy.

"Every time we dredge, we film the ocean bottom in front of the dredge bucket. We use a 16 mm camera enclosed in a special titanium sphere mounted in a basket between the two powerful spotlights. To learn how nodules are spread out on the ocean floor. Or to identify the obstacle that might have caught and damaged the bucket. Which happens once in a while. The pressure at these depths is tremendous. More than five tons per square centimeter. That's why we cannot use TV cameras. Once we mounted a sphere with a small hidden defect in the casting. It came back up flat as a pancake. The camera inside too, of course.

"Sometimes, for fun, we lay raw eggs in the basket. An eggshell is porous, so we always get the whole egg back. But inside, the white and the yolk has been compressed to such a point that is has turned hard as a rock... and half its initial size.

"The collected nodules are analyzed by scientists. We have two of them aboard. They are nice guys. But they have strong personalities and thus, they argue all the time:

-"You see, dear colleague, this nodule is at least two hundred million years old."

- "No. You are wrong as usual. It must be at least four hundred millions years old."

- "It is much younger. How can you talk such nonsense ?"

Thus they argue all day long. Everyday.

The nodule is then cut in half with an electric saw. At the center you find either a fish bone or a shark tooth. Objects that fell eons ago in the cold silent depths and created a nucleus to start the crystallization of the dissolved metals.

One afternoon, an exceptionally large potato was found in the upcoming bucket. The scientists handled it with respect and awe.

And the bickering also started immediately:

- "You see, this one must be at least one billion years old."

- "No. It is much younger. Around four hundred million years. But the nucleus must be a large object. Like a whale tooth."

- "You're crazy. Whales did not exist then. Feel the weight. It is pure metal. You must have found your degree in a soap box."

It was dinnertime and the arguing persisted throughout the meal. The crew started to show interest for this unusual potato. The boredom of shipboard routine helping, the men soon split into two groups. Each supporting one of the scientists.

The captain, also a gambler always looking for opportunities, went to fetch a cigar box. To collect bets from everyone. Whale tooth or not whale tooth ?

The betting money collected was stuffed in the box and the entire crew followed the two experts to the laboratory.

It took half an hour to cut the nodule in half. Everyone was shoving at the cabin door to get a glimpse of the perspiring scientists.

Then one half of the nodule fell on the floor with a loud thud.

Total silence followed. Dead silence.

At the center of the nodule they found... a gasoline engine spark plug."

Tahiti Blues

MARLON'S TAHITI BLUES

The letter arrived on a Thursday :

"Beverly Hills, October 2
Dear friend,
I have to call on you again.
You must have heard about the hotel being closed. I want to reopen it for business. But I'd like you to have a look first. Please try to find out also why I've been having continuous problems on the island.
So please go to Tetuara. I'm expecting your report.
My best regards to Poerava.
Marlon Benton."

I read the letter twice. With great pleasure.

I am in love with Marlon's atoll, Tetuara. I love that island the same way you may feel for a woman. With passion.

An atoll is a separate world. Another world altogether. A place of communion with nature.

An atoll is the only land created by life. By living organisms.

It is not the result of the clashing of tectonic plates. A fragile jewel like an atoll cannot be associated with such a brutal act.

An atoll is the offspring of a secret plot of the noble elements of our planet. The fire of the bowels of Earth place the embryo; patience of time shapes it; water and sun nourish it; and the wind weans it.

Look at the Pacific Ocean. Huge. Vast. Too vast. More than half our planet.

Deep also. More than three miles on average.

A small weak spot in the cold dark depths of this endless body of blue waters. And the fire of genesis will slowly, patiently push the magma until it breaks through the surface of the ocean. This volcano, a huge mass, will then be taller than the biggest mountain in North America.

The volcano will eventually run out of strength, will become extinct. Its weight, so huge and so lonely, thousands of miles from any continent, will make it sink. Slowly. Inevitably. Until it disappears again into the seas.

But a small detail will change everything. Tropical

corals will discover a perfect habitat on this submerging land.

A solid base. Lots of light. A warm ocean. And oxygenation, provided by the endless surf produced from steady trade winds or storms of the Roaring Forties.

And the volcano will keep sinking, and the coral will keep growing. Generations and generations on top of the calcium, skeletons of their fathers and ancestors.

Soon no more trace of the volcano will be visible— just a ring of coral.

A lagoon will then be born.

The endless sea will then cuddle this fragile jewel with loving care. Stroke it with its waves. Feed it with its oxygen. For centuries, ages, eons.

But an ocean, just like man, can turn insane, crazy, violent. Especially when it feels too hot.

In its folly it will then try to destroy, to maim, to mutilate what it had nurtured with such patience and love. This insane fit is called a hurricane.

Monstrous waves, like tremendous sledges, will pound, break, smash the fragile colorful underwater gardens. The nursing swell, which has become a destructive ram, will lift entire reef sections up, throw them on top of others; will grind the coral and beautiful shells into fine powder.

Worn out, the seas will quiet and expose a view of desolation in proportion to its size. On the wounded reef large mounts of debris will stink in the reappearing sun.

A few years later, the rains will have rinsed the salt out of these dunes. Sea birds will joyfully discover this new roosting place. Their droppings will provide nitrogen and the coconut and the seeds washed on these new beaches will find adequate soil. A few years later the dunes will be green with vegetation.

An atoll just has been born.

The reef will continue to grow, will heal itself, and shall become the protective barrier for these fragile sand islands. Without these ramparts made of billions of living polyps, the swell would just take one swallow of these storm leftovers.

This is where the ambiguity of an atoll lies : Every time the ocean has a fit and tries to destroy, this action creates more debris that only makes the atoll larger. It has thus become a living being that thrives on its surroundings, adapting to its moods.

Lots of time will pass. Lots. Eternity.

Then, some day, some men, lost on the endless sea, crowded in a fragile canoe, will be washed onto these remote shores.

They will worship this saving land. They will learn to survive on these few acres. Learn to peacefully cohabit on it. They will figure out how to dress, how to eat, how to heal with only coconut and fish and live that way for centuries on, for generations.

More time shall pass, and a big ship will appear. As big as a village.

Men, white like clamshells and bearded like devils, will come ashore. To barter fish and nuts against shiny, useless and inedible things, but also metal, unknown to the natives. Then they will return to the floating village, leaving the gaping natives...

But before disappearing, one of the bearded devils will open the large barrel on deck. The time it takes him to drink a couple of ladles of water will be sufficient for a few mosquitoes to start the short flight toward the atoll.

From that day on, the nights will be less pleasant. And the children will have diseases and wounds.

Other tall ships will pass. Many more. Some curious. Some hungry. Some mean or merciless.

One ship shall invite all the men from the atoll to a big feast aboard. And when they hungrily throw themselves on the unknown delicacies displayed on a table in the cargo bay, the hatch will spring shut.

The men from the atoll will then agonize in the horrors of slavery in guano mines of Peru or on Australian plantations.

The children of the atoll will grow up without fathers.

They will collect the mother-of-pearl shells to provide shiny buttons for silk shirts. Harvest coconuts to supply factories at the other side of the world that make oil and soap.

But the never-ending genius of technological man soon will invent new, more efficient ways to manufacture buttons and soap. The people on the atoll will have to leave their island. They have forgotten how to feed, dress and cure with island resources only.

The delicate atoll will then be abandoned.

It will use this respite to heal itself, to regenerate its shell stock, to regain some harmony with the sea birds.

Not so long ago, Marlon Benton came to Tahiti.

You all have heard of Marlon, of course.

Yes, he's the famous movie star. I shall not bore you here enumerating the many, many movies that made him the worldwide icon.

What happened to him in Tahiti is a rather common scenario.

Marlon, spoiled by riches and success, and certain to have thoroughly tasted all pleasures of life, was soon disconcerted by the femininity and innocence of our island girls. Of those who have remained natural.

He fell desperately in love with Tina, the hotel receptionist. He married her and started a new family.

As his universal fame was getting to be quite a burden, he decided to utilize this unexpected quirk of fate to escape the Hollywood dream machine.

Sheer luck made him stumble onto the atoll of Tetuara.

The first time he discovered, from an airplane window, this ring of small islands enclosing a lagoon of a thousand shades of blues and greens, Marlon experienced his second Polynesian love. For he had finally found what he was unconsciously seeking since boyhood.

Marlon is always ahead of his time. A very sensitive man, he was already a fervent ecologist at a time when civilized man still believed he could rape his environment freely. That nature was there to be consumed, just like tissue paper.

It turned out to be quite easy for him to acquire the entire island. At the time, it had no commercial value. People on our sparsely populated islands did not understand then that the peace and solitude of isolated islands, and the liberty these permit, are for the rest of the over-crowded world the ultimate, almost inaccessible luxury.

Marlon spent the following years building a small run-way and a life base on the atoll.

He also built a twenty-bungalow resort hotel. To in-duce wealthy tourists to share with him some of the huge expenses such an undertaking involves.

Twenty bungalows that could house forty people. The maximum amount of guests Marlon would allow on his island. To not disturb the peace. To not stress the envi-ronment. Especially to not bother the hundreds of thou-sands of seabirds, the real owners of the atoll.

Marlon surely was not taking any risks. Forty people on more than three thousand acres of coconut forests, in a five-mile diameter lagoon, were not what you would call an environmental impact.

Still he took extreme care to integrate this little hotel into its surroundings.

As only island lumber had to be used, he built a sawmill to achieve this. Any chemical products, insec-ticides or wood preservative were banished. All non-or-ganic garbage, like plastics or used engine oil, was shipped back at great expense to Papeete.

He did not bow either in front of urban fashions and habits. His hotel offered only the basic necessities : A shelter against the weather, a flush toilet to crap in, a bed to sleep and make love on, a mosquito net to do it in peace, simple healthy food in the restaurant, and a strong cooler for ice cold beer and drinks.

All this in one of the most enchanting surroundings anywhere in the world. A site of indescribable virgin beauty. Any intelligent and sensible being would be overwhelmed with wonder.

Should your quest for pleasure be in the noise of discos or in the futility of social ascension, then please do not come to this island. You shall only meet disappointment there.

For a few years Marlon lived happily with his family on the atoll. But, like some creeping vine, the call of celebrity, the financial reality and the temptations of modern comfort caught up with him. Called him back to California.

This is when our roads crossed. He suggested I take care of the island.

I accepted. With great pleasure.

Thus I became one of those few privileged ones. Privileged to be the master for more than a year of a very small but immensely beautiful empire.

I hope that I never abused my power. I hope never to have hurt any of the fifteen Polynesians who so pleasantly shared my year of exile. A year without raising my voice. A year without meanness. A whole year where the problems seemed to disappear every night into the ocean with the sunset.

Of course, tensions could develop. Which would be normal. A few people living together in a closed circle are apt to get cabin fever.

But the art of running such a community is to get the feel. To be able to feel when tensions are coming, when personalities are about to clash.

You have to interfere right away. You have to keep communications open. You must take the necessary time to listen to everyone. To accept each person the way he is, with his qualities and faults. To make absolutely sure never to exclude any member of this group.

All other problems, be they mechanical, logistical or meteorological, were minor compared to the harmony of our small isolated family.

Thus, the main endeavor of the head of such an isolated community is to be a good confessor, almost a psychiatrist.

But I must admit that my success was due essentially to the extreme tolerance of the Polynesian mind. Their still very rural mentality, based on laws of mutual respect and good sense, did much more to soothe tensions than my fancy educated talking.

Then it was time to leave. It was sad to part from this life of serenity.

But my daughter had to go to school. And the sand and lagoon are so bright that my blue eyes were slowly getting blind.

It was also about time for me to leave for other reasons. I was starting to feel too much at home in this sheltered world, far away from the hysteria of the industrial chicken-farm that is today's modern world.

The atoll can be like some dope. Peace and serenity are addictive.

Had I stayed longer I would have become one of these 'atoll maniacs', one of these beachcombers who drift from island to island doing small jobs. They are quite easy to spot when they stop over in Papeete. Tanned, if not burned by the sun, they smile endlessly and greet everyone. If you start talking to them, it will last for hours. They have all the time in the world.

I keep in my brain a little treasure box full of sweet memories. My year on Tetuara provided many of these :

The daylong walks on the deserted beaches counting turtle nesting sites, which look like tractor tracks leading to areas where the sand had been up heaved.

The endless canoe rides on the lagoon to visit the bird nesting islands regularly. To ensure that nothing and no one would disturb them. That no predators would scare the thousands of fluffy white down balls that were the baby boobies.

The nights spent alone on the mirror lagoon or on some lonely beach, waiting to catch some poachers. Nights that I would end up feeding beer to those same poachers. Poor guys who had spent a whole day sailing over, hoping to better their lot with a couple of sea turtles that city people pay outrageous prices for. At least, while we got drunk, the turtles were safe to lay their eggs.

The memories of the full moon nights, when every palm frond shines silver. When the shells on the sandy bottom of the lagoon are more visible than in daylight, and the moon reflects itself in this mile long mirror.

But the image that remains etched in my head is the sight of the atoll when you fly toward it. After one hour of watching only the dark blue waters of the vast Pacific, it appears like some fata morgana. As if the gods had laid an impressionist painting there. A palette covered with every possible shade of blue.

And the snow white sand gives these pastel colors a luminosity, a brilliance that is almost painful to watch.

I call it the painful blue. The Tahiti Blue. It burned my eyes. Etched my brain.

The letter from Marlon had awakened the atoll virus in me. I hurriedly packed my bags, took wife and kid, and left for Marlon's magic island.

Jean-François, the manager of Air Moorea, insisted on flying the plane, not being certain about the condition of the runway.

An hour later, the atoll appeared on the horizon, like a sapphire lying on a blue cloth.

The plane aligned with the short runway, a narrow strip of coral that looked too short for our twin-engine plane. But Jean-François, a real expert in bush landing, managed his landing smoothly and stopped next to the lagoon, almost on the beach.

A Tahitian, about forty years old, bare-chested and wearing a worn straw hat, came running to open the doors. I recognized Matahi, friend and companion of the old days. We greeted and kissed one another with real joy. He has been watching the island alone for the last eight months.

It took an hour to unload the freight. Then Jean François took off, waving frantically from the cockpit. We watched him get higher, farther in the sky, until he became a tiny spot that disappeared in a cloud.

The silence wrapped us in. We were alone. All alone. Again. Finally.

Our stay lasted six weeks. I sent my report to Marlon on Christmas Eve.

Here it is :

- Moorea, December 23rd.

Dear Marlon,

We just returned from the atoll. Mission accomplished.

I know you are a busy man, thus I'll try to be precise and to the point.

But certain causes are rather subtle, and I shall extend those.

You can always use this as a guide for your future island managers.

Pleasant reading.

Your first wrong move was to ask your Los Angeles accountants to take care of the island.

These gentlemen, who are very competent on the stock market and in keeping your books, are going to try to run your island the way one manages a canning plant.

Their priority will be maximum efficiency, balanced books, and profits.

Trusting them with your island was just like taking your mistress to your banker and saying :

'Here she is; make a profit out of her!'

These highly efficient professionals gladly accepted, against proper remuneration, of course. They then ap-

plied standard procedure : Find an experienced manager to whom they, in turn, can trust the island you just entrusted to them.

This manager will be chosen according to their personal criteria of excellence. Which means that he must be very much the way they are. He must speak English (they can understand him). He must hold fancy diplomas (like them). He must have references (someone tried him out for them). He must be married (that, strangely, means he is stable). He must have held a similar post (he is experienced). He must show past profits (he is efficient). He must be French (no work permit required).

They did find one. His name is André. He ran a small motel north of San Francisco. He made some profit. He is married. He has fancy diplomas. He is a French citizen. What more do you want? They found the rare bird. They are pros. They congratulate each other.

But André has never seen an island. He has never seen a Tahitian. Doesn't talk one word of their language. Never read a book about the place. The only fish he ever saw was on his plate, with sauce amandine. He knows nothing about the tropics. Nor about the sea. But he is 'dynamic and efficient'. Now, that's important.

The new manager and his wife arrive on the island as conquerors. Very rudely, they chase away poor Cornelius, who has been holding the atoll together for two years. They do not even take the time to ask him to explain the thousand and one little secrets that facilitate life on an island. Those details you painfully learn after hundreds of mistakes.

But they must get rid of the former authority right away to take things in hand. Anyhow, what could such an old island bum teach them anyway; doesn't André have many diplomas?

André is not a bad guy. But he owes much of his success to his wife. Very ambitious, she nudges him a little every day, corrects him continuously.

André is actually a sensitive man, who listens to others, tries to understand them. Who wants to go his way through life without imposing too much on others? But his wife, whom I shall call 'Madame', analyzes this modesty as a weakness. With her, you have to be a 'winner'.

Everything in her way must be moved, destroyed, demolished, pulverized. Zapped, like she says.

She is one of these new French women. One of the most amazing mutations of the twentieth century.

As a young man living in Paris, I was then ravished by the French girls. Their charm, their femininity, their elegance, their taste was unequalled in the world. I still today remember the laughter of these charming ladies, their ponytails held with silk scarves, dressed in cute little 'tailleurs' and designer boots.

The entire world was in admiration for the assurance and joy of these women. Men from all countries were arriving, hoping to find a spouse among these wonders. Especially Americans.

Twenty years later, I return to France. I'm aghast. Almost no more elegant women. No laughter anymore. Hardly ever a smile. Rare are those who even appear feminine.

I see mainly bitter women, bossy women, even aggressive women. They walk clicking their heels like Marine sergeants. Their hair is cropped short. If you try to talk to some, they look at you in a suspicious way, almost hostile, as if they wanted to say, 'What do you want, hungry male chauvinist?'

No more nifty dresses, no more ponytails. Gone is the laughter. Gone are the smiles. The assurance is replaced by bitterness. The femininity by unisex. What the hell happened in France during those twenty years???

I got the answer one late night at the bar of the hotel George V, the snob meeting place on the Champs Elysées. A British journalist, correspondent for Reuters, had the kindness to explain it to me after his third whisky.

He said that Europe has the habit of copying what is done in the States. Usually with a two year delay. So does France. The woman's lib movement of the late sixties was no exception.

But what had been a fairly short lived and rather marginal movement in the U.S.A., dreamed up by spoiled and frustrated suburban housewives in Long Island country clubs, became a real institution in France.

Because the rhetoric was picked up by the political parties of the left, who were seeking a new jingle. Their old, old one, 'the communist 'struggle of the classes', was just not credible anymore in this new society of plenty.

The myth of the 'oppressed woman', exploited and repressed, arrived just on time. In France it turned into a collective hysteria. A real new religion. Blasted on the air by the new television channels. Fanned by the youth upheavals of the sixties. Then picked up by all major political parties in quest of new votes.

This intellectual tantrum, created by some New York alcoholic or lesbian suburbanites, was made into a regular national institution of France. It is taught in schools, is graded, and even has its own government department, 'the Ministry of Feminine Condition'. Authentic!

Which is actually quite saddening. All this feminist mentality does is infuse women with the same complexes that have plagued certain racial minorities in industrial countries for so long.

It tries to make women feel like victims. It tells them they are exploited. That they must hate man, this 'despot'. It must also convince them that they are exploited sexually, and that if you make love to them, they should be compensated for it.

Women, who have always so artfully used their favors over the centuries to get the icing of the cake, must now completely relearn their roles. Learn how to make sure they get 'correctly remunerated for their sacrifice'. If you really look at it closely, all this women's lib is only the introduction of prostitution mentality into the bosom of family life and human relations.

And it will inexorably lead these women to the very margin of society.

No? You don't believe so? Well, go ask the forty million American single women or divorcees.

And the fate of the Frenchmen will look more and more like that of the American urban male :

In the morning, on the way to work, you gotta fight the traffic. At the office, you gotta fight your way into the elevator. At work, you gotta do your infighting against the ambitious young wolves. At noon, you gotta fight for a place at the cafeteria. In the afternoon, you gotta fight more against the infighters. After work, more fight in the traffic. And this, everyday, all year long.

And finally, you get home. Exhausted. Dead tired.

You beg for a bit of rest. A little peace. Because you have fought to exhaustion all day to pay the installments of your wife's social ascent : The split-level suburban home. The imported car. The stereophonic color TV with projection screen. The fake Chippendale furniture. The remote controlled automatic VCR. The Wedgwood china. The Apple computer for the kitchen recipes. The super microwave. The Cuisinart (all this just to make hamburgers). The designer dresses. The exerciser bike. The tons of make-up. The gallons of perfume. The Vuitton luggage. The electric curler, hair dryer, eye lens sterilizer, vibrator, pealing wax heater, and the most chic—the latest electronic gadget.

You mentioned rest ? Peace ? You're dreaming, man. No rest. Now you must fight with your wife. Because, a liberated women, she wants to be better than you, over you, ahead of you. You're just a dirty exploiter, you who dare look at her with a 'dirty greedy look'. You should be ashamed, no?

Poor man. You now know which were the factors that promoted the incredible progression of homosexuality in the seventies. Maybe these men were seeking among themselves the affection that their wives refused to give them?'

OK, Marlon, excuse my mental wanderings. But I wanted you to understand which mold shaped Madame... And I do know you love this kind of story.

Because Tetuara, your atoll, your dream, this last virgin land, is now in the hands of such an egocentric ambitious woman. She'll run it through her husband, whom she controls.

When women talk about equality, they understand taking charge.

Madame understood immediately the potential of the island. Absolute power.

She decided to install here the perfect world as she saw it. She was going to introduce what the world lacked most : Class ! Madame was an expert on class. Wasn't her great-aunt a member of nobility? She repeated it often enough to André to justify her superiority.

She asked him to create a secretarial position on the atoll. Thus she would be part of the company.

There never had been any paper work on Tetuara. To whom should you write anyhow? Everyone saw everybody else at least ten times a day. If you needed something, you just called Tahiti on the radio. The office there took care of whatever little writing had to be done.

No matter, from now on, whoever committed a breach of rules or a fault was notified in writing. But this memo also had to be delivered. To do that would not have been worthy of Madame. So she hired an office boy.

She also quickly became aware that the Tahitians did not seem to fully realize how important she was. She, the manager's wife, the manageress.

Well, this was because these people were not really 'civilized'. She would have to import personnel more aware of 'the values of society'. Europeans.

Didn't the bar need a manager? Wasn't a real chef a necessity? And the boutique? And the gardens? Didn't they all need 'competent' people?

So she made André hire. Bar manager and assistant for the tiny ten-seat thatched hut on the beach. A shop manager for the miserable little room offering a few dusty tee shirts and lava lavas.

A housekeeper to run the maids she just couldn't understand. Maitre d' and wine steward for the restaurant. And a head gardener to take care of the coconut trees and pandanus shrubs that had been growing alone for ages.

She flew to Papeete to hire them herself. To pick the ones who were the most reverent to her.

And even more were hired. Two receptionists to greet the dozen clients arriving twice a week. And many more gardeners. Madame had now decided to transform this sand and coral atoll into a tropical garden. Flowers meant class. Sand and coconut trees were just not adequate. Nature had to be modified. Transformed. 'Improved'. Molded to her vision of perfection.

She thus succeeded in increasing the permanent population from fifteen to fifty two people.

But all these classy people had to be housed. The village was for 'Tahitians' and quite crowded. So guest bungalows had to be used.

And your small hotel, which more than tripled its employees, now had only twelve bungalows available for its clients. Fifty employees for twenty guests. Real class indeed.

The island mood was changing too.

All these new arrivals turned the fragile community into turmoil. It split into two groups right away. Tahitians on one side; expatriates on the other. No more harmony. No more big family where everyone respected the other.

Almost none of the expatriates had any experience living in such a confined area as a small atoll. After a few weeks, tensions inevitably arose. They started yelling and screaming, something you never do with Polynesians. They resent it as an insult.

The Tahitian community then just pulled back into its shell. Created its own universe to maintain its values. They still did their work, but without joy, without laughter.

They didn't joke anymore with the customers. It was forbidden now. It was incorrect, Madame said. They did not stay after work anymore to sing, to play the guitar and the ukulele. They didn't invite clients to go fishing with them anymore. They stopped sharing with them the little secrets of atoll life.

No more flower leis patiently strung for the ladies. No more long talks showing the family photo album. No more teasing the gentlemen. No more soft tropical village life. All replaced by the vanity and futility of Madame's new world of classes, castes, manners. The Tahitians were now mere shadows of themselves. Real zombies.

And to drown the pain caused by this new modern world they started drinking all the booze their pay would buy.

Madame did not notice. Could not notice. She did not know the community before. She had no yardstick to compare. She thought what she saw was usual. Thus the endless drinking and its ensuing dramas only confirmed her suspicion : She, the apostle of 'civilization', had to bring her message to these 'natives'.

She was having to struggle more and more to maintain her society. The expatriates were fighting more and more among themselves. She had to replace them constantly. The employees did not obey anymore; their respect was gone. Even her husband started showing signs of disobedience.

She had to fire girls who insisted on being familiar with the clients. And she had to get rid of another woman, who persisted in doing her work with her baby, even daring to seat him in the 'duty wheelbarrow'.

Yes, Marlon, this is the type of hell that this woman managed to introduce on the atoll. She just wouldn't realize that nothing will separate a Polynesian mother from her newborn child. That this baby sitting in a wheelbarrow under the coconut trees is just the image our visitors travel thousands of miles to find. That her requirements that the guests wear long pants and jackets at night in the restaurant, so she could play social queen, was a drag on them. Nor did she realize that chasing away the kids fishing or swimming in front of the bar was saddening the clients.

You must think that I made all this up.

No. Not at all. Our busy bee wrote it all down. Kept every memo. Filed them neatly. In the rusty file cabinet in the room next to the reception. Madame's former headquarters.

Matahi and I had to kick this cabinet, slam it, and shake it to get it to open. It seemed the salty air and the humidity of the great ocean had united to prevent us from resurrecting these painful memories.

It is also in these archives that I found the story of the 'visit' to Tetuara of the yacht called Eagle of Jamaica. It describes well the mood on the island at the time.

This world famous racing yacht was equipped with the most modern navigation systems : satellite navigation, Omega, GPS, you name it.

Before leaving the harbor of Papeete to sail to Honolulu, the captain entered the longitudes and latitudes of his departure and his destination into his super computer. It gave him the 'great circle' bearing to follow. With care, he traced this route on his Pacific Ocean chart. No obstacles showed on his route to Honolulu. His felt pen made a thick black line, and your atoll is a tiny flyspeck at that scale, much smaller than the line that covered it. Thus he could not see Tetuara.

The following day, at three o'clock in the morning, your fringing reef was decorated with the Eagle of Jamaica, laying on her side, the fastest, most modern, most expensive racing sailboat in the world. Its hull was in shreds.

At dawn, Matahi, on his way to pick up the fishing nets, discovered this mass lying in the breakers. The atoll notified the Navy in Papeete, who decided to send a helicopter.

Madame then got all excited. Such a classy boat on 'her' island! Finally, a visitor worthy of her kingdom had come. Even an Englishman! She had to greet him properly. Maybe this was finally going to permit her introduction into High Society. She who is so refined !

She stormed into the kitchen and ordered the chef :

- "Quick, quick! The helicopter is coming! I need hot water. And tea bags! And cookies! Quick, quick!"

The chef, pissed off at Madame since a long time and in bad mood that morning, said :

- "I'm the chef! I don't wait on people !"

- "But it's a real emergency! Quick, quick!"

- "I'm chef ! I don't serve!"

Seeing the chef nervous, she could very well have made hot water herself and gotten the cups. But it would have seemed demeaning to her. She answered :

- "I shall tell André. He will chase you off the island !"

- "You can take your pimp and stuff him up your a...!"

Screams. Hysteria. The assistant chef has to be awakened just to make hot water. At great expense, the hotel will lose one of its best chefs ever. All this to allow Madame to receive the distinguished shipwrecked captain in style. He who is actually an even bigger fool than she is. Three million dollars spread out on the reef was ample testimony.

But it was a charming tea and the conversation was of a very high intellectual level...

The more time passed and the more Madame became severe, the more tense everyone got. Hundreds of dis-

missal letters and memos show how hysterical the people on the island were becoming.

That is when the God Neptune, or maybe it was the God Hiro, decided that enough is enough. He felt sorry for this little Eden he had created with so much love.

How could he keep on being an impassive witness to the macabre ballet of this ambitious insane shrew ? Maybe he was mad at Madame for never having really watched the symphonies of blue on the lagoon. Nor having felt touched by the tenderness of the boobies for their fluffy chicks. Nor felt infinitely small and futile under the star-studded dome of the tropical night. Maybe she never even noticed it.

The Gods rebelled. They filled their chests and blew a cyclone. A small hurricane. Just strong enough to cleanse the beloved island of Madame's perfect world. A world of another time and place.

Not strong enough to hurt anybody. But strong enough to wash ten bungalows out to sea. Enough to drown the colorful flowers with saltwater. Enough to push over a thousand coconut trees—but you have millions. But enough to close the hotel and send everyone home.

Enough to return Tetuara to its serenity.

You see, Marlon, our islands are ruthless with those who do not respect them.

Look at the Gambier Islands and their empty cathedrals. Look at Norfolk Island with its empty stone carved penitenciary. Look at the disaster on Bikini atoll. Look at the Easter Island statues. All are relics of empire dreams. All are also monuments to the sufferings of a kind and gentle people.

Our islands shall always be fatal to the arrogant, to the despot. Because they will very soon be confronted with themselves. Like in a trap. It's unavoidable.

Maybe this permanent lesson of modesty is at the root of the kindness and the softness of Polynesian communities.

This, Marlon, is what happened on your atoll.

Oh! Another thing. I almost forgot.

Way at the bottom of the rusty file cabinet, I discovered the financial balance sheet for one year of Madame's perfect society : A clear loss of five hundred and thirty two thousand eight hundred and sixty three dollars.

Dreams of the likes of Madame are very, very expensive too.

As usual, you are the one who paid for them. Poor Marlon.

Hope to see you soon."

Six weeks later, Marlon flew to Tahiti to take a look at the damages on Tetuara.

The next morning, at the end of the Tetuara airstrip. he stood a long time leaning against the nose of the small plane, motionless, looking at the long white sand-bar that stretched where once stood a row of cozy little thatched bungalows.

After a long, long silence, he turned my way and with a mischievous smile uttered, while nodding his head :

- "Sure looks clean!"

Alex W. du PREL
Opuhi Plantation, Moorea,
South Pacific

About the author :

Born in 1944, Alex W. du Prel is an expatriated American living on the islands of Bora Bora and Moorea, next to Tahiti, since 1975.

After studies in France, Germany, Spain and the USA, he worked as a civil engineer on large construction projects in the Caribbean and South America. At that time, he also built a thirty-six foot yacht that was to become his home for twelve years.

To keep a freedom of travel, the author (a civil engineer) engaged in many, different professions : surveyor, welder, movie actor, mechanic, hotel resort chief engineer, construction superintendent, hotel manager, translator, cook, government consultant, island manager, journalist and editor.

He sailed single-handed across the Pacific Ocean in 1973, then spent a year visiting many isolated islands and atolls of the Central and South Pacific, some uninhabited.

In 1977, he built and operated on the island of Bora-Bora the "Bora-Bora Yacht Club", a small hotel that soon became the meeting place of all long distance sailors of the time. He sold the Yacht Club in 1982 and settled as a farmer, consulting engineer and freelance journalist on the island of Moorea. From 1985 to 1988 he managed Marlon Brando's atoll of Tetiaroa.

A truly international man, a specialist on South Pacific affairs and Polynesian societies, the author speaks six languages and writes in three.

Since 1991, he is the founder and editor of *TAHITI-Pacifique Magazine*, the only French language monthly news magazine in the South Pacific.

Alex W. du PREL is married to a Tahitian lady and has three children.

Books by the author
Le bleu qui fait mal aux yeux (French, 8 Tahiti print runs).
- *Le Paradis en Folie* (French, 8 Tahiti print runs).
Blaue Traüme (German), Tanner Verlag, Zurich Switzerland, 1992.
Verrücktes Paradies, (German), Tanner Verlag, Zurich Switzerland, 1994.
"G.I.s in Paradise, the Bobcat project", with Tom J. Larson (1995).

This book has been a bestseller in Tahiti (a tiny market) and has also been published in German by Tanner Verlag, Zurich, Switzerland, as well as a small private printing run in Japanese.

The cover

Acrylic on canvas paintings by **Philippe Dubois**. This French painter, longtime friend of the author, is living on the island of Moorea (10 miles from the island of Tahiti) since 24 years. He is certainly the most popular painter in Tahiti, an island famous for its artists *(among which Paul Gauguin and Edgar Leeteg),* yet he is still unknown outside of French Polynesia. His paintings, reasonably priced, are available.

If you are interested in his art, feel free to contact the author <alex-in-tahiti@mail.pf > who will forward your message.

DID YOU ENJOY THIS BOOK ?

Want more ?

A second book by the same author is ready

« **Crazy Tahiti Paradise** »

French language éditions of these books ;

Le Bleu qui fait mal aux Yeux
and
Le Paradis en Folie

are available online.

Thank you for your interest.

CPSIA information can be obtained
at www.ICGtesting.com
Printed in the USA
FSHW021949310719
60600FS